C.A. VARIAN

THE OTHER WORLD

Contents

CLOUDFELL
LORD ARGALL'S MANOR
COURT OF KNOWLEDGE
EMERA
WHISPERING FOREST
THE SANCTUARY OF HEALING
PORTAL
WHISPERING FOREST

THE WORLD OF ECROMOS
EMBERGUARD
TIMERSTORM
COURT OF CHAOS
COURT OF HARMONY
COURT OF COURAGE
BLAZE'S FARM

CHAPTER ONE

Elianna

"Some say the worst thing about having cancer is knowing you have it, but I'd argue that the worst part is throwing up my perfectly good pizza because of the meds." A few people in the circle nodded, murmuring their agreement before I continued. "My name is Elianna Foster. I'm nineteen years old, and I have stage IV thyroid cancer that has invaded my lungs like Battlestar Galactica."

Sometimes, I wondered if jokes were my only defense mechanism left. If I could keep everyone laughing, they wouldn't notice how scared I was—or worse, how lonely I felt. It was easier to make light of my cancer than to endure the painful silence of knowing it would ultimately kill me. The thing about attachments—friends, boyfriends, even fleeting acquaintances in the group—was that I couldn't hold on too tightly to people who might vanish at any moment. I didn't want to give them the chance to hold on to me.

The entire group, twenty people sitting in a circle, called out, "Hi, Elianna" in unison, some giggling at my nerdy comment. I bowed from the waist and sat back down, stifling a cough and adjusting the oxygen cannula in my nose. The one thing I didn't say out loud was that I would not survive this disease. I didn't need to say it. Everyone in that meeting had some form of cancer. All our lives felt like they were on borrowed time.

"Are you going to use the key?" asked one of the younger guys in the circle. I believed his name was Liam, but I couldn't be sure. From listening to his conversations with the others, all I knew was that he had leukemia and was sixteen years old. I didn't often get close to anyone from the circle of the sick. I didn't want to go through the heartbreak of losing them. My swaggering, nonchalant facade almost cracked when I was asked about the controversial key, but I quickly fixed my expression and secured my walls back into place.

The Keys of Ecromos were the only way to open the portal in the Shrine of Solstice and cross into the realm of the fae. However, keys weren't given to just anyone. For a human to cross over, she had to be female, dying, and left with little hope for her life in the human realm. If it came down to survival, women who crossed into the realm of the fae would be relieved to be there—glad even—and wouldn't fight what was expected of them. They wouldn't resist returning home. The hopelessness required to make that choice made it an impossible decision for me.

Some called the Shrine of Solstice holy—a mercy from ancient gods who took pity on dying humans. Others whispered that it was nothing more than a gilded slaughterhouse, where the fae dressed up captivity in the trappings of salvation. In Brookwood, stories about Ecromos circulated like wildfire—rumors traded in grocery store lines, late-night radio programs, and conspiracy forums online. No one could prove what was true because no one ever came back.

According to the stories, it was rare for fae females to bear offspring. This genetic mutation was causing their race to decline and potentially die out. Fae healers could cure human diseases, but the infertility among their females was a problem they couldn't solve. Furthermore, most of the children born to fae couples, if any survived, were male.

I knew little about Ecromos, aside from the rumors, but it certainly seemed like the fae needed to mate with humans before their people, and the magic they held, died out for good. While I empathized with their plight, I was also only nineteen years old. I had no interest in settling down and having children, even if I didn't have to leave my world to do it. It felt unfair, to be burdened with such a choice at such a young age.

Aside from the rumors and legends, the portal remained a mystery to humans, as did the world beyond it. Since no one ever returned, speculation ran rampant about what happened to those who entered. The door into Ecromos allowed humans to travel only in one direction. Some claimed that human women were used like cattle, forced to breed half-fae children for the wealthy. Others speculated that each woman received a key matched to a single fae male, her fated mate, who would be waiting for her on the other side.

The idea of a soulmate was easier to accept than the worst-case scenarios that haunted my mind. However, it was still a reality I wasn't ready to face. I was uncertain if I would ever feel prepared to be a wife or a mother. The real question wasn't whether I was ready, but whether being compelled to have children with an unknown male was better than facing death.

Regardless, I hadn't decided what I would do if the time came for me to choose between leaving my home or dying. With the cancer in my lungs making each breath a struggle, I knew I had to make a choice soon. Ready or not, the decision weighed heavily on my mind, a constant source of anxiety and fear. The fae had the potential to cure my cancer and grant me a near-immortal lifespan, but only if I sought their help before it was too late. Once I reached a point where only machines could keep me alive, the opportunity would be gone. I had to decide—*soon*.

Forcing my expression into something less melancholy, I cleared my throat. "I haven't decided if I'll use the key. I know it's unlikely I'll beat this illness, but we don't really know what lies beyond that door. And once you cross, you can't come back." I smirked, attempting to project a confidence I didn't feel. "I'm not sure I'm ready for that level of commitment. I've never been one for commitment, anyway."

A few people laughed, but some remained serious, making me regret the joke.

I didn't recognize the middle-aged woman who stood up, but her grimace made her lack of amusement clear. I shrank back inwardly, even if my face didn't show my discomfort. "At least you have that option. Women my age have no choice but to face death. There are no keys offered to us, no chance at hope. If there were, I would gladly take it. Maybe you should consider that before dismissing your one chance to live."

I left the cancer support group feeling less than stellar. Using the key was a very personal decision, and I understood that. However, the woman's comments still stung. They made me feel like a spoiled child. Maybe that's what I was, but at only nineteen years old, was I really expected to view the decision as anything other than an overwhelming burden?

Despite all the unknowns, the possibility of surviving my fate and being healed was enticing. Perhaps the woman from my group was right, but I just wasn't there yet. The current treatments wouldn't cure me, but they were keeping the Grim Reaper at bay.

Tapping my hands on the steering wheel of my red sedan, I listened to the radio, trying to will the stranger's words out of my mind.

My mother, Elizabeth, was already setting the dinner table when I arrived home in Brookwood. My family hadn't always eaten together, but my mother insisted on it ever since my cancer had spread to my lungs. From that point on, I was required to sit at the kitchen table every night, listening to my father talk about his clients and my mother discussing only the gods knew what. I loved my parents, but it was as dull as watching television on static. Nonetheless, I endured it. They would miss me when I was gone, so sitting through family dinners every night felt like a small price to pay. They were great parents who loved and cared for me through it all, so I would have given them anything I could while I was still there to do so.

My mother smiled when I walked in, her blue eyes always bright despite the shadow of grief behind them.

"How was the group?"

Shrugging, I grabbed a buttered roll before plopping down in a chair at the table. The woman's comments hadn't helped the nausea that constantly plagued me, but I was determined to eat anyway. "Same as always. Aside from Jerry dying, the conversations don't really change."

My mother paused, looked up as my father, Peter, walked in, and then sat down at the table before responding. "Is anyone planning to use the key?"

"Mom." I tried to muster as much annoyance in my tone as I could.

It seemed the same repeated conversations would continue at home as well. The way she constantly brought up the key made it feel as though my mother had given up hope for me. Once I used the key, my chance of staying with my family would vanish. I wasn't ready to give up just yet, even if my mom seemed to be. Was becoming enslaved really better than death? I didn't know all the facts about what awaited me on the other side of that door, but becoming a sex slave or merely a breeding animal were two very real possibilities. I wasn't sure if either of those was an improvement over the alternative.

The worst part about holding that key wasn't the power it promised, but the commitment it demanded—a one-way ticket to nowhere. Humans like to keep their options open—college majors can be changed, apartments sublet, and boyfriends can be dumped. But Ecromos? That was permanent. You couldn't peek through the door, test it out, and simply slide back into your old life if it didn't fit. That finality made me queasy in a way even the chemotherapy never had.

My mother raised her hands in supplication. "Alright. I'm sorry. I just want you to think about it, okay?"

Leaving her task behind, she sat in the chair next to me and took my hands in hers. "Sweetie, you know I love you more than anything. I'm not giving up. But using that key could end your suffering and give you the chance at a full life you could never have here."

Just in case it was possible for me to feel any worse, my mother managed to make it happen. She never did it on purpose, but it didn't lessen the pressure her words put on my already slouching shoulders.

"Elizabeth," my father interjected, frustration clear in his voice. "Let it drop. She has enough on her mind."

"Alright. Alright." My mother squeezed my hands one more time before returning to the kitchen counter to grab the plates.

"It's okay, Dad. I know I need to make a decision. It's just difficult when I don't have all the facts."

Pulling off his glasses and rubbing his eyes with his

hands, my father looked exhausted. "You don't have to make one right now, Firefly. The key will still be there for you later. Let's focus on getting you better for now."

I nodded, but I knew my father was trying to pacify me. The key might still be there for the moment, but I didn't have much longer, and I knew it. The coughing and shortness of breath were getting worse, as was the feeling of hopelessness. If I had many more years ahead of me, I didn't know if I could handle spending them as sick as I was.

Forcing down my dinner, aware that the medication would make it come up later, I settled back into my role as the sick daughter, rolling with the punches so I wouldn't make my parents worry more than they already did. I may have been the one living with cancer, but we were all helpless.

The key taunted me as I lay in bed that night. The intricate skeleton key was an antique gold, enchanted with the magic of the fae, and it had been given to me on the day my doctor confirmed that my cancer had spread to my lungs. I had placed the key beside my television that night and hadn't touched it since.

The air seemed to thin, and the pain in my chest grew. The key beckoned to me like the call of a siren. All I would have to do was grab the key, go to the Shrine of Solstice, and place it in the lock. If the stories were true, I would be taken to Ecromos and healed. I would never see my family again, nor would I know if survival in the human realm had been possible, but the cancer would be gone.

Maybe, if the best of the rumors were true, I'd find a soulmate there—someone to share the rest of my much longer life with. Even with a new family, the thought of living through the loss of my parents was too much for me to bear. It was an impossible choice.

Each key was said to link one fae male and one human female, making them destined for each other. I wondered if that was why the key sometimes seemed to glow from within, as if the fae were trying to get my attention. But what if I didn't like him? What if I wasn't attracted to him? Even worse, what if he were cruel to me and treated me like a prisoner, like no more than a breeding mare? I didn't have the answers to those questions, but I needed them to decide whether leaving my world was better than staying.

I lay in bed for hours, contemplating this, as the pressure in my chest grew tighter. Some fates, I realized, were worse than death.

A harsh cough caught me off guard as I rested. I doubled over on the bed, my breathing becoming increasingly ragged. I watched the key through watering eyes, and it flickered, emitting a brief flash of light I had only seen a few times before. It lasted only a moment, but I knew it was real and not just a trick my oxygen-starved mind was playing on me. With determination, I climbed from my bed, grabbed the magical object, and felt the unmistakable power surging through it and into me. The compulsion to use it was palpable.

"You've been MIA for like three days, Elli. Where have you been?" My best friend, Kiera Harris placed her hand on my forehead, pretending to check for a fever as we sat in the university's coffee shop. I took classes from home, realizing it was mostly a waste of time. Kiera got to live on campus and experience all the things I would never be able to. It would have been a lie to say it didn't bother me that I was missing out on the experiences others took for granted, but dwelling on it wouldn't change anything except my mental health.

I shrugged. "My cough got worse, so my mom insisted I stay in bed and eat awful canned soup while watching reruns. You know she'd prefer it if I never left the house. It wasn't my finest few days, but I did get through two smutty novels while pretending to study."

Kiera laughed, taking a sip of her nonfat latte. "Elizabeth's going to find your dirty book stash one of these days and set it ablaze. Just you wait."

Rolling my eyes, I tossed a straw wrapper at her. "Like you've got room to talk. I borrowed all those books from you."

"You're so full of it," Kiera replied with another laugh, but her expression turned serious a moment later. "When do you guys head to Kinderside to see the new specialist?"

I had been trying to avoid thinking about it. The new specialist would say the same thing as the last eight had. It wouldn't change anything. It would only remind me of how much I had endured. "Tomorrow, I think. I don't even keep track anymore."

The night before any doctor's appointment was always stressful, even though I'd lost hope for remission. I settled into bed, pulling out one of the steamy novels I kept in my side table drawer, and opened it to where I had left off. I didn't know why I bothered hiding them from my mother. At nineteen years old, I was technically an adult, but my parents still treated me like I was twelve. That said, I didn't mind being taken care of.

After reading for hours and fantasizing about the attractive character in my current book, who was adding to my growing list of book boyfriends, I fell asleep with the paperback resting across my stomach.

Tightness gripped my chest, and I struggled to draw in enough air, pulling me from sleep. Gasping, I reached for the buzzer my parents had installed next to my bed a few months earlier, pressing it repeatedly to wake them. My heart raced, pounding against my ribcage, each attack feeling like it might be my last. Thankfully, it only took seconds for my mother to rush into my bedroom, followed closely by my father.

"I'll call the ambulance," my father said as he dashed out of the room to grab his phone.

My mother leaned over the bed, securing the oxygen cannula to my nose and reaching for my inhaler on the side table. I inhaled the medicine, but it provided no relief. I continued to struggle. The air in the room felt inadequate, even with the oxygen tube. Spots danced in my vision, and with a moment's clarity, a desperate thought crossed my mind. I looked at my mother, urgency in my eyes, and extended my hand toward the metal object flickering next to the television. "Get the key."

CHAPTER TWO

Elianna

The golden key in my mother's hand was the only sign the first responders needed to know where to take me. It was a scenario they were familiar with. With the sound of the siren piercing the late-night silence, the ambulance raced toward the Shrine nestled within the Haunted Mountains, the exit leading to the hospital fading into the distance. Grief was replaced by numbness, filling my ailing body with every mile we drove down the darkened roadway.

It was ironic how numbness and fear wore the same face. I had learned to protect myself with small detachments—a practiced shrug, a joke, a refusal to plan—because planning meant hoping, and hoping meant breaking. Cancer had taught me that attachments came with expiration dates, but this felt different: this one-way ticket to Ecromos carried a finality I hadn't been trained to accept. The ambulance's rhythm matched the ache in my ribs and the steady slide of my life toward a place people whispered about, like something from cautionary tales. I had always refused to need much. Tonight, that refusal felt both cowardly and necessary.

My parents hovered over me, holding my hands and whispering words of encouragement, but all I felt was nothing. Nothing, aside from the pain in my chest and the lack of oxygen in the space around me. I would never see them again. It wasn't a reality I could face, so I pushed it to the back of my mind, trying to pretend I was simply going to yet another hospital visit. This way, the fallout of my decision wouldn't hit me until it was too late to change my mind or take it back. By the time I allowed those feelings to flood back in, I would be stuck inside the realm of Ecromos, forced to either confront them or be too preoccupied to think about them. Either scenario felt better than letting doubt fracture my shaky resolve now that I had finally decided.

When the key was placed in my hand, just as the ambulance approached the Shrine, the light within it flashed faster, more frantically, as power surged through it and into my palm. The key's light wasn't just brightness—it was pressure, a warmth that threaded through my bones. It made my fingers hum and filled the air with a metallic taste of promise. For a moment, I could have sworn the metal had a heartbeat of its own, something ancient and patient, as if it had waited a very long time to be touched. The tug was not just a portal-pull. It felt like both an invitation and a challenge, as if whatever awaited on the other side wanted more than my body. It wanted me to choose who I would be once the choice became irreversible. I was terrified of that kind of ownership. Still, secretly, somewhere beneath the panic, a small part of me was curious.

It was as though touching it compelled me to follow through, as if someone on the other side was begging me to come to them. I felt the portal's pull with every fiber of my being, but the hesitation I had been suppressing grew stronger as well.

By the time the vehicle parked and my stretcher was rolled out onto the roughly laid pavement, tears came out in sobs, uncertainty lacing every ragged breath. "I've changed my mind. Mom?" The pain in my chest made the words difficult to articulate. "*No. Let's go back to the hospital.*"

When my mother looked at me, silver lined her eyes, but she shook her head, crushing my heart. "Sweetheart, please. This is the right decision for you."

My father faltered, pulling the stretcher to a stop. "Maybe we should wait, Elizabeth. Clearly, this isn't what she wants. She shouldn't be making this decision while she's in distress."

Another round of violent coughing hit me, my body betraying me when I needed it to cooperate the most. I needed my parents to have faith that I could recover and to take me to the hospital instead. I needed more time. I always needed more time.

Wiping her eyes and setting her jaw with renewed determination, my mother yanked on the stretcher, forcing it to roll toward the Shrine again. "We have to do this now, Peter. If we wait," she hesitated, her voice shaking with her sobs, "if we wait, it may be too late. You know the rules. They won't take her if she's too far gone. Even now, what if she's too sick? We have to do this *now*."

I didn't argue out loud. My body was in too much turmoil for my words to hold any weight. I knew my mother was right, even if I didn't want to admit it, even if I wasn't ready to leave them. The truth was, I would never be ready.

"What's it gonna be, Elianna?" one of the first responders asked as he locked the stretcher in place.

It was my mother who answered. "She has to go. We have to do this now, while she still can." My mother leaned over me, cradling my cheeks between her hands. "Sweetheart, your dad and I would do anything for you, and this is something we must do. We love you too much to let you sacrifice your life for more time with us." I shook my head, tears streaming from my eyes as I glanced from my mother to my father, committing their faces to memory. "After all the years you've suffered, this is your chance to be free from the pain. This is your chance to be happy."

My father moved closer, taking me by the hand. "Your mother's right, Firefly. It's time."

Even though my mind knew my parents were right, my heart couldn't accept what they were saying. I nodded, or at least something that could've been mistaken for a nod.

The Shrine of the Solstice loomed before me, a white structure that stood in stark contrast to the dark mountains surrounding it. The stretcher began rolling toward the open entrance again, up the ramp designed for people like me—those who couldn't walk in by themselves. *Dying people*. The white marble of the building gleamed in the candlelight, making the entire interior glow with a magical aura.

Although I had read all about the Shrine and had been schooled in how to reach the door, I had never been inside. I had never even been in the parking lot. The walls were covered with mosaics depicting the setting sun, landscapes, and plant life, all glimmering in the candlelight and seemingly alive.

The door, a cerulean blue, stood against the back wall, framed by large sconces with flames that were larger than usual, almost as if they were enchanted. They probably were. I stared at the door, focusing on the antique lock, hoping it would somehow signal what I should do next and reveal my fate on the other side. But it remained silent. It just stood there, challenging me.

My eyes darted from my parents to the first responders, and the feeling of desperation grew within me again. "Mom? I don't want to do this." I reached for my mother's hand, which gripped the railing, and pulled it toward me. "Please, *Mom.*"

The two men who brought me there looked uncomfortable as they observed me and my parents, waiting for someone to make a decision. They didn't speak. Instead, they focused on my oxygen and vital signs, waiting patiently for what would come next.

My mother squeezed my hand, the key pulsing against my skin. Then she pulled me into a hug, but her eyes were distant. "I'm not saying goodbye, Sweetheart. But I know this is the right thing for you to do, and you know it too." My body shook with the force of my sobs, but I didn't argue. I was in too much distress to make the right decision for myself anymore.

When my father leaned over me and wrapped his arms around me, my crying only intensified. "You're gonna shine in Ecromos, Firefly. Just wait and see."

I knew my father believed what he'd said, but I wasn't so sure. I was uncertain about everything. Still, I glanced up at the first responders with my tear-stained eyes and nodded, feeling less confident than I tried to appear. My parents held my hands as the oxygen was removed, my lungs straining without it, but I didn't object.

"You need to turn the key, Sweetheart," my mother

said, releasing my hand and nudging it toward the door as the back of my stretcher was raised into a sitting position.

Without my cannula, the growing panic inside me made my breathing more erratic. I had never felt so powerless, not even when I had received my diagnosis, even as the diagnosis had worsened. My father reached behind my back, helping to lift me from the bed while the first responders supported me on weak legs. I lifted the golden key to the antique lock, my hand trembling as it approached the door.

Violent coughing seized me again, my chest tightening without the extra oxygen. I doubled over as they held onto me, the key slipping from my fingers and falling to the ground, clanging loudly as it hit the floor.

The next moments were a blur, my oxygen-starved brain processing too slowly for things to make sense. I coughed against my father's chest as he cradled me on the ground, while my mother reached for the key. The surrounding scene spun, but it felt like only a moment passed from when I dropped to the floor to when my mother slammed the key into the lock and the door creaked open.

Beyond the doorway was a white void. I couldn't see what lurked behind the light, unsure if the brightness stemmed from my weakened body or if that was truly what I was about to enter.

My mother placed the key back into my hand, kissed my forehead, and gave me a warm smile before stepping aside. I stared into the void as my father and the first responders lifted me, setting me down just inside the opening. The last thing I saw before the door closed, separating me from my parents and my world, was the silver behind my father's eyes and the moment my mother's strength shattered.

As soon as the lock clicked into place, I collapsed, the light enveloping me as I went unconscious.

I wasn't sure how much time had passed since I had been left inside the doorway, surrounded by an endless sea of white. I also couldn't tell if I was still alive. Snippets of visions flashed in and out of my consciousness: the feeling of hands touching me, images of people surrounding me, and dis-embodied voices. I couldn't focus on anything in particular. I was too weak, too exhausted. While the coughing had subsided and my breathing had become easier, I didn't have the strength to analyze why. Maybe I was dead. A moment of panic washed over me before oblivion consumed me once again.

When I woke, the room was stark and empty, save for a small bed, a table, a sink, and a toilet. The walls were a sterile white, as were the sheets and the gown I was wearing. The lack of color made me wonder if I was still in the spot where my parents had left me when they closed me into the portal. There were no windows and no door handle. I was trapped—*imprisoned*—but too confused to panic just yet.

My chest no longer hurt, and I took the first deep breath I'd been allowed in over four years. Maybe I *was* dead. A whimpering sob rose in my throat, but I pushed it down as sounds echoed from the other side of the door. Crouching in the corner, I waited for the door to open, waiting for some sign of whether I was in the other world or if my time alive had come to an end.

"Oh, good. You're awake." An older woman walked into the room with a tray balanced in her hands. No, not a woman—a fae. She had to be.

Iridescent wings, like those of a dragonfly, were tucked against her back as she set the food tray on a small table near the wall. Her skin was tinged with lilac, her ears slightly pointed. Aside from the color of her skin and the obsidian of her eyes, her face resembled that of a human. Even her thick black braid, which fell down the center of her back, was reminiscent of women in the human world. It made me feel self-conscious about my own hair, or lack thereof, which had only just begun growing back after my chemotherapy, and was barely long enough to tuck behind my ears in a chestnut pixie cut. Smoothing my hands against my hair, I watched my visitor.

Although the fae's sweet voice and sugary smile were disarming, my heart raced in my chest. I had never needed my mother as much as I did at that moment. "Where am I?"

The fae froze for a moment as she prepared a cup of tea, surprised by my question. When she turned back around with the steaming mug in her hands, the saccharine smile remained on her face. "Well, you're at Lord Argall's manor in the Court of Knowledge, Miss. My name is Hiedra. I will be tending to you while you're here. What's your name?"

Her statement made my stomach clench, the implications reminding me of the fears I had harbored before using the key. "My name is Elianna..." I hesitated, scanning the room. "I thought the key would bring me to my mate, the one with a twin to my own. Where will I go when I leave here?"

I looked around the room for my golden key but

didn't see it anywhere. They had taken it. An ominous feeling crawled over me, seeping into any part of me that had previously held hope.

Hiedra shrugged and reached for the bowl of soup. "I know nothing about a mate, Miss. You came to us rather sick, and it took a lot to heal you. But as I understand it, you'll be with a new master as soon as you're all fixed up."

The word "master" hit me like a bullet to the chest, bringing my worst fears to life. I was a prisoner.

CHAPTER THREE

Blaze

Pulling on the reins of my horse, I urged the animal to go faster. My dark shoulder-length hair whipped free from its leather tie as Shadow galloped across the plain. I'd been watching the silver key flicker for the past few months, but it had only just become more insistent. When it shined from within that morning, and didn't fade immediately, I knew my mate had arrived in my realm. My hopes and dreams were coming true, and I couldn't wait to get to her. With a few days' worth of supplies in the saddlebags, I'd left my cottage that morning to head toward the portal entrance in the Whispering Forest. I knew my fated companion would need more, but there were places along the journey back to my lands where I could get her whatever she needed once I had her safely astride my horse. The distance between us put a strain on my chest, the mating bond pulled tight.

The Court of Harmony spread behind me in quilted fields and lavender belts, farm smoke lifting in thin blue ribbons where dawn fires had been coaxed to life. I'd left a sprig of rosemary tucked in Shadow's bridle—an old Harmony ward against ill chance—and the little copper bell on her breast strap chimed now and then, a soft note that kept wood-spirits from dogging our heels. The road stones glittered faintly with sun-runed sediment, the kind masons baked into our highways after the war to keep travelers from losing their way in fog.

Expansive woodlands separated my home in the Court of Harmony from the bordering Court of Knowledge. The location of the portal between the fae realm and the human realm was an isolated place, tucked in a cave deep inside the forest.

The Whispering Forest earned its name honestly. Pines breathed like a choir when wind moved through their needles, and the low trees were furred with a moss that released silver dust if you brushed it with your boot. Here and there an old redoubt from the Four Courts War hunched under ivy, its arrow slits black as old wounds. Fireflies weren't fireflies at all but wisp-moths, their bodies lit from within by witch light they stole from fungus caps. Even the boundary stones wore history—runes for warding, for return, for mercy—carved by hands long gone to ash.

Because of its isolation, only a handful of guards and healers remained there to receive the human women as they arrived. My mate would have been retrieved once she'd arrived through the portal that morning, and then would have been brought to the temple. Once there, whatever affliction had caused her to leave her world would have been cured. Fluttering in my core, excited energy filled me as I urged Shadow to move faster along the path.

The Sanctuary of Healing was nearly a day's ride from my lands, but I had no intention of stopping until I got there, not unless I absolutely had to. Even though I was destined to be with her, whoever she was, I knew there were female snatchers in my realm. The thought of her being taken loomed over my mind like a dark mist. There were those who made money by stealing humans once they crossed the portal and selling them to those who could afford them. The longer it took for me to get to her, the more at risk she was.

I thought about her the entire way. Thought about what she looked like and what her name was. What had made her decide to come to my lands in the first place? I'd held onto my hope for a key for years, and had only just been given one, never imagining it would find me a mate. My relief was immense. After decades alone, I would finally have a companion, a lover, a friend. That was the hope, anyway. If she would have me.

Arriving at the Sanctuary of Healing just before sunset, I secured Shadow's reins to a nearby tree and approached the building, eagerness surging inside and filling the lonely parts of me.

The place of healing was manned by the priestesses of the combined courts, who saw after the human women once they crossed through the portal, the location of which was nearby. The Sanctuary wasn't grand so much as inevitable—four white apses like open hands, each faced toward one Court, each banded with its Court-mark: Courage's bronze knot, Knowledge's ink-black quill, Harmony's wheat sheaf, Chaos' crimson fractured sun. Wind chimes hung in the eaves—bone and glass, whispering prayers in a dozen dialects. The air usually carried the bite of feverfew, the sharpness of star-mint, the earthy weight of willow bark—remnants of the healers' work. I had been told the scents clung to their halls like a second skin, that the building itself breathed with quiet labor. But none of that greeted me now. Only stone and silence.

My excitement faded as I approached the entrance but heard no sounds of life coming from within. My hearing was powerful for a fae, but I heard no voices, no movement aside from the wind making its way through the trees. Something wasn't right.

"Hello? Is anyone here?" Even though I'd never been to the location before, I knew it should've been filled with people, both the healers and the sick. Swallowing down the dread building in my throat, I took silent steps through the front door.

Sounds of someone breathing heavily broke the silence as I moved through the marbled front chamber. Following the direction of the sound, I entered a room on the side of the foyer, a hunched figure appearing in the corner. At first, I wondered if it was my mate, but that hope was quickly dashed when I noticed the shape of small wings pressing against the inside of the female's hooded cloak. It was one of the healers, a veil faerie.

She didn't seem to notice me coming in, or if she had, she was trying to pretend that she wasn't there, trying to make herself invisible. "Hello? Are you okay?"

Still not understanding what was going on, I approached the female slowly. Her body stiffened, her breath catching. Lowering myself to her level, I scanned the healer's lilac face. "Are you okay?" I repeated.

She shook her head, dark eyes lifting to meet mine. "Someone took them," she said, her voice cracking with emotion. "Someone took all of them."

Ice flooded my veins as I helped the female off the floor. Her lilac face was reddened, tinged with unspoken pain. "Who took them?"

Not answering right away, she shuffled across the room and lowered herself into a chair. "I'm not sure. My sentries went to the portal when we received the alarm that someone came through, but they never returned. I went out to look for them, but there was no one there."

My face became as twisted as my stomach, fear and rage blending into an emotion I'd never felt before. "Take me to the portal."

Since it was only a mile away, the healer, Tansy, and I traveled there on foot. I needed to see the portal for myself. If my mate left anything behind for me, if those who'd taken her left any tracks, I needed to find them. I needed to find her.

The moon was high in the sky by the time we'd arrived, my heart getting there before my body did.

The light of my torch flickered off the black stone walls, creating eerie shadows in the darkness. Although the entrance into our world was glamoured on the human side to resemble a door, it was nothing more than the rear stone wall of a cave on the fae side. There was no way to cross into Iloya from Ecromos, nowhere for me to place the key that was inside my pocket. I'd never been to the portal before, but the humans were truly trapped once they entered through it. There was no doorway, no way for them to go back. Aside from the stone wall of the cave, there was nothing there. *No one.* Even if daylight had been upon us, there would have still been no trace of a human woman, or the sentries who'd gone to retrieve her.

I rubbed my temples, panic growing inside my

chest. My need to run after my mate, to tear the world apart until I found her, warred inside me. "Does this happen often, Tansy? Females being stolen."

I already knew the answer, but I asked anyway.

With her hand cupping her mouth, Tansy paced, the healer seeming at a complete loss of what to say or do. She was just as powerless as I was. "This last happened a few weeks ago. King Jolar sent more guards since then, but we received an urgent message earlier today about a group being attacked on their way into the city. Most of my sentries abandoned their posts to help the victims... Now I'm wondering if it was all a ruse to take the female."

Swearing, I kicked the gravel at my feet. "Any idea who's doing this? Even if you aren't sure, tell me your theories. I need somewhere to start. I have to find her."

Panic gave way to desperation. It bled into my voice. I'd waited so long for a mate, a companion, and I couldn't lose her, not like this. *Not ever.*

Scanning the darkened forest, Tansy seemed to look for something neither of us could see. "They couldn't have gone far."

"What makes you say that?"

The winged female rubbed her palms against her long skirts before signaling for us to head back to the Sanctuary. I followed. "The humans who come to us are sick—*really* sick."

The thought of my mate being so ill that she'd been forced to leave her home was like a knife to my chest, even though I knew it was the one thing that had brought her to me. She was mine, and I was hers. I felt it in my very soul. The thought of her suffering shattered my spirit. I couldn't let her sacrifice lead to more pain, to a miserable future when she'd taken such drastic measures to survive. To whatever end, I had to find her, and had to bring her happiness. Repeating the vow in my head, I waited for Tansy to continue.

"Without the quick work of healers, many of these human women would die. Wherever they took her, she would have needed a healer, and quickly."

I nodded, realization settling into my mind. "So, they wouldn't have taken the chance to steal her if she couldn't survive the journey. They must be close." I quieted for a moment, the sounds of wildlife filling the silence as we walked. "Is there somewhere I can take you, Tansy? I don't want to leave you here if you'll be in danger."

Shaking her head, the healer pulled back the side of her cloak, showing me the gleaming dagger that was strapped to her side. "Don't worry about me. Someone must stay here in case another human comes into the portal and needs my help. Hopefully, my sentries who went to the crash site are safe and return soon. Until then, I'll keep my blade at my side. Your mate needs you. I'll be fine."

I didn't like leaving Tansy alone in the middle of the forest, but I knew she was right. My mate needed me, so I couldn't waste any more time. Arriving back at the stone building, I thought about my plans, the task ahead of me so much bigger than I'd planned for when I'd left my lands that morning.

Knowing my mate couldn't be far didn't narrow down my search all that much. Ecromos was large, the four Courts of Chaos, Harmony, Courage, and Knowledge spreading out across the continent. The closest court, the Court of Knowledge, was covered in vast forests, dangerous forests. I would walk to the ends of the world for her, but I needed to know what direction to aim first. "Tansy, do you know the locations of the nearest brothels?"

When I first asked the healer for the location of the nearest brothels, her confusion was apparent on her lilac face, but it only took a moment for her to realize my reasoning. As unfortunate as it was, if females were being stolen, the flesh trade would have been the obvious place to look. There were many females who worked in the brothels because they wanted to, but there were just as many who had no choice. It was the seedy underbelly of the realm that its rulers ignored, mostly because they made handsome profits on the trade themselves.

I stayed away from brothels. Not that I didn't desire a female's touch, it was just that I wanted the female who touched me to do it because she wanted me, and not because she wanted my coin. There were few options in our realm, with nearly all the females of consenting age either mated or in the flesh trade, so it wasn't an experience I'd had more than a handful of times. Occasional females over the decades, needing the same release as I did, with no desire for commitment, had invited me to their beds, but it had been many years since I'd had the skin of a female against my own. Maybe I would've caved one day, tired of using my hands, and paid for someone else to touch me, but I hadn't yet. Instead, I spent the lonely nights waiting for my key to shine with the light of the female who was destined for me.

The thought of her out there in the realm without me created a tightness in my chest, making it difficult to breathe. Digging my heels into Shadow's sides, I urged the horse to pick up speed. Maybe, since my mate had arrived in Ecromos sick, she'd not yet been thrust upon the flesh market to give her time to heal, but that concession wouldn't last. Eventually, those who'd stolen her would expect their risks to reap a reward. I had to find her before that happened.

CHAPTER FOUR

Elianna

My heart dropped into my stomach as my worst fears flooded through my mind: fear of being a slave instead of someone's partner, fear of being no more than breeding livestock. The possibility of having a soulmate, someone to share my life with, seemed merely a fantasy after Hiedra's last words.

"What do you mean by a master? I thought I'd be meeting my mate."

The winged female smiled, but it didn't disarm me as it had before. There was something Hiedra wasn't telling me.

"Many fae nobles need heirs, Miss, but that's not for me to explain." Pushing the tea toward me, the servant ended the questioning. "Now eat up. I'll check back with you when it's time for your bath."

Slumping back onto the bed as soon as the door clicked shut, tea and food were the last things on my mind. I was being held in a lord's manor and would eventually be sold to another master. Someone owned me, would own me. If I'd known I would be expected to breed like a farm animal, I wouldn't have used my key. It was too late now. There was no way to go back home. But regret wasn't the same as surrender. Even if the key had locked me into this gilded prison, my mind was still my own. I'd learned in chemo wards and waiting rooms how to sit still while secretly cataloging everything—the way nurses rotated shifts, how long IV bags took to drain, and which doors were never fully latched. If survival had taught me anything, it was how to notice patterns. And noticing meant options, even here.

The fae female was lying. There was no question in my mind. Hiedra claimed to know nothing about my key but seemed to know quite a lot about my being sold to a noble to birth his heirs. No matter what my current circumstances were, I didn't believe I'd been given an enchanted key, a key that flickered and thrummed with power when I touched it, solely for the purposes Hiedra claimed. Something didn't add up. I didn't have a way to know the truth just yet, but I was determined to find out.

Just as she said she would, the winged servant returned a few hours later, waking me from an unintentional nap. The sound of the door opening startled me, and for a moment, I'd forgotten where

I was.

"Time for your bath, Miss Elianna." Hiedra still wore her disarming smile, but I wasn't fooled by it. I knew the servant was keeping secrets. "Are you feeling well?"

I nodded as I sat up in the bed, my head still foggy from sleep, but my lungs were pain-free and cycling air with no trouble. "Did they cure me? My cancer?"

Turning the blankets down and setting slippers on the floor, Hiedra reached out a hand to help me up from the bed. "That they did, Miss. You're much better now."

I wasn't so sure about that. Just because my cancer was cured didn't mean my life would suddenly be better. I hated the thought that they thought curing me meant owning me. Survival wasn't the same as freedom. If they believed I'd trade one cage—my failing lungs—for another, they didn't know me at all. Still, a life without cancer? It was something I couldn't imagine, even in my wildest dreams.

"How long will I be kept here before I'm sent to my new home?" The word home tasted like poison on my tongue, but it didn't seem to faze Hiedra. The female had undoubtedly seen my scenario play out many times before.

Climbing out of the bed, I slipped my feet into the white satin slippers and let Hiedra shuffle me out the door. "I'm not sure, Miss. Until then, since you're feeling better, you'll be moved to the shared quarters with the other human females."

Other females? I wondered how many women were there, and how many would be sent away like me? No one had mentioned an auction to me yet, but I was smart enough to know I'd be sold to the highest bidder. The situation only seemed to get worse. It burned the back of my throat, souring my empty stomach.

We walked through the large manor house side-by-side. The halls were empty of others, aside from the occasional fae guards. Unlike the stark white of the room I'd been kept in, the rest of the manor was rich with color. The hallways from my room to the bathing room were painted in a rich emerald, artwork of beautiful landscapes hanging throughout. I scanned the passages as we passed, trying to memorize the layout of the home in case the time ever came when I could get away. Every turn we took, every door that groaned on its hinges, I memorized like I used to memorize formulas before a test. My body might still be frail, but my mind was sharper than they realized. If they expected obedience, they'd underestimated the stubborn girl who used to argue with doctors about treatment plans.

"Will I ever meet the lord?" I didn't want to meet him, the male who'd probably stolen me, but I needed to understand more about the world, more about my future. Since he was the one who would sell me, he was someone I needed to learn more about.

The servant didn't answer as we approached a set of double doors framed by two guards, the fae males dressed in black uniforms, gleaming swords strapped at their waists. One male nodded at my escort before opening the door for us to enter.

The bathing room was enormous, with several soaking tubs throughout. "Zoe," Hiedra called out to a blond woman who was folding towels near the back wall. "Elianna is being moved into your quarters. Stay with her until I return."

The blond woman, Zoe, smiled, but it didn't meet her eyes. I didn't get the feeling that the emotion was directed at me, however. With a curt nod, Hiedra turned and left the room, saying nothing else.

"Old bat," Zoe muttered under her breath, I barely stifling a snicker. I looked forward to talking with the other women, to finding out if their keys were missing as well. Something inside me told me I'd been stolen, that I wasn't where I was supposed to be, but I still needed proof. Maybe we could get our keys back and escape together.

"So, they snatched you, too, huh?" Zoe asked, her tone full of empathy.

Although I had already known it in my bones, my stomach dropped at the confirmation of my fears. "I've only been here for a day—I think. So, I'm not even sure where I'm supposed to be."

"None of us are supposed to be here. Lord Argall

traded in his key a long time ago. He doesn't need a mate, not that it keeps him from screwing the humans he steals. Ever since trading in his own key, he and his cadre have been sneaking in and snatching us before our mates can get to us. He's probably looking for you right now, your mate, I mean." Zoe shrugged. "Mine probably gave up on me a long time ago."

Her words should have crushed me, but instead they lit something small and furious inside. If my mate was out there, I refused to believe he would stop looking. And if he did...well, then I would just have to learn to save myself.

Still, the walls seemed to close in on me, claustrophobia making my breath become too shallow. I scanned the room for a way out, but there wasn't one, not with guards blocking the only exit.

My mate was looking for me, but my physical link to him, my key, was gone. I wondered about him, wondered what he was feeling. Had he yet realized I'd been taken? Knowing I may never meet him shredded my heart into pieces. "What does he want with us? Why would he risk so much to steal someone else's mate?"

Zoe grimaced, leading me to the pool closest to the vanities lining one wall. "Same reason as in the human lands. He makes a lot of money by selling women. The slave trade is very profitable in Ecromos. He doesn't take women often, though. Not to my knowledge, anyway. From what I've been told, they take enough to keep the trade profitable, but not enough to cause an uprising. Although I'm sure there are plenty of males tearing the realm apart looking for their mates. Lord Argall's healers get us nice and healthy before sending some of us to the brothels and others to the highest bidder. It's been going on for years."

Taking off the sterile white gown, I sank into the bath, my stomach churning. Zoe followed. "So, what was your reason for using the key?

I cycled a breath, thoughts of my parents flooding my mind. I already missed them. "Stage IV thyroid cancer that spread to my lungs. I wasn't ready to make the decision, but I got really sick a few nights ago. *Really* sick." I paused, stealing my nerves. "It was an impossible decision. I changed my mind on the way there. Multiple times. My parents really thought it was for the best, especially my mom. She was more than persuasive when it came time to open the door. She ended up having to unlock it for me."

Zoe's powder blue eyes grew larger. I shifted uncomfortably in the warm water, wondering if I'd said something wrong. "That may be why you were taken. If you don't unlock the door yourself, it doesn't trigger your key's twin as quickly as it should, at least not right away. Unless I misunderstand the process."

I couldn't be angry with my mom. Neither of us knew the consequences of my not opening the door myself, and it wasn't like I'd been capable of doing it myself anyway. I'd been too busy coughing and fighting for breath when the key fell. My mom had been forced to pick it up. With burning behind my eyes, I turned back to Zoe with more questions than I was ready to ask. "They told me I'm going to be sent to a new master. What about you?"

"Some of us, like me, are kept by Lord Argall to work in his brothels. Others are sent to auction. With your arrival, there are twenty-one women who share our wing of the manor, but I'm not sure how many will be sold off soon. There's a bit of a revolving door here."

We were quiet for a while, and I wondered if I would be better off going to whatever master purchased me, rather than staying with the rest of the human women under the lord's control. I only hoped that my new owner was kind and wanted me for himself, instead of forcing me to work in a brothel. If I stayed with Lord Argall, it sounded like working in the brothel would be in my future.

Returning to the bathing room an hour later, Hiedra escorted us to the section of the manor that was reserved for the human women. The servant was tight-lipped, leaving no opening for us to ask questions.

I paid close attention to the path as we walked. There were fewer decorations in the halls between the bathing room and the human quarters, less extravagance, making it more difficult to map out.

The double doors to the rooms for the human women were monitored by two fae guards, both donning swords and stern expressions. One of them opened the door immediately, a young male with deep brown hair and hazel eyes, who looked only the human age of twenty. He barely made eye contact with the two women whom he was a part of imprisoning.

When I settled down that night in the small room I would share with Zoe, my mind swam with all the information I'd been given that day. I still wasn't sure what my obligations would be while I waited to be sent to my new owner. With my arrival, there were twenty-one human females under Lord Argall's control, a few of whom were promised to other males but had yet to leave. In my case, as seemed to be the case with several of the women, the lord was expected to heal us and restore our health, since many of the human females came into the realm too sick and usually too thin.

As Zoe had earlier stated, there seemed to be a revolving door at the manor, with new women arriving to replace those who had been auctioned off or purchased in private meetings. With the lack of females in the realm, there was always a market for them. There were always males who'd either never found a mate or simply desired more women at their disposal.

To my dismay, most of the human females who were in Lord Argall's keep were all but sex slaves. They either spent their time in the brothels, or in their quarters, the shared rooms providing them with the opportunity to rest and find a sense of camaraderie with the other women. After over five years of cancer, I had never been with a man, and I didn't want my first time to be as a slave, used for my body and nothing else. I wondered how long I would be there before being sent to the new location, fear of ending up in the brothel filling me, creating a toxic pit in my stomach as I tried to fall asleep.

I curled onto my side, but I didn't close my eyes right away. Fear was heavy, but underneath it, a stubborn ember smoldered. I had been sick for years and still managed to cling to life. I could cling to myself here, too.

CHAPTER FIVE

Blaze

Tansy, the Healer on High at the Sanctuary of Healing, was familiar with the nearby brothels since she had to treat the females who worked in them regularly. The parchment she'd given me with the directions to the closest of them sat tucked inside the pocket of my cloak as I rode deeper into the forest. With every muscle in my body taut, I ignored my hunger, my exhaustion. I'd left the isolated structure quickly, the urgency to find my mate overpowering my own body's needs, but my energy waned with every mile. I hadn't slept in more than a day, but thoughts of my female's suffering, and the burning desire to find her, kept me going.

As night turned to day, even with every jolt of Shadow over the tree roots in the Whispering Forest, staying on the saddle became a battle I was losing. The wild lands separating the kingdoms were teeming with animals, roving bandits, and magic. Every so often, the trees themselves shifted with a groan like bones, their roots flexing just enough to block or reveal a path. Once, when I was a boy, a stag made of moss had stepped out of these same shadows and vanished like mist before my father's eyes. You never forgot that the forest watched you back. So, although I could hardly keep my eyes open, it was the last place I wanted to stop and rest. Not when I was traveling alone.

The forest seemed endless, the fresh scent of the evergreens and the choir of wildlife crowding my senses. Dense and ancient, its canopy was dominated by fir, spruce, and pine trees, and sparkling light danced between the branches, allowing for a patchwork of sprouts to burst from the brittle leaves on the ground below. Curling creepers held onto the trees, and a medley of flowers, which grew in a sprinkled and disorderly fashion, protruded from the otherwise unchanging view. It was easy to get lost in the beautiful chaos of it, but I kept my eyes ahead, urging Shadow to follow the same path that had been trampled by others.

Here and there, half-buried boundary stones jutted from the undergrowth, carved with wheat sheaves and ink quills entwined—a relic of the treaty that once bound Harmony and Knowledge. Moss had filled the carvings with green fire so the old marks glowed when the light hit them.

Without a view of the sun's location through the thick canopy, I often worried I was going in circles. I slowed Shadow periodically, making slashes on occasional trees with my dagger, just in case I passed the spot again. So far, I hadn't. The disharmony of sounds, mostly belonging to varmints and birds, echoed in the air, making my skin crawl. Occasionally, just below the sounds of the wildlife, I could've sworn I heard someone calling my name at just above a whisper. I knew it was merely my own fatigued mind playing tricks on me, but it still filled me with uneasiness.

The smell of smoke and the muffled sound of voices alerted me that I was no longer alone. Slowing Shadow's steps to remain unseen, I encouraged my horse to move close enough to see who was making camp. Shadow's movements were near silent, nothing more than a ghost on the wind, as she crept toward the unsuspecting individuals. Roasted meat intertwined with the scent of burning wood, my empty stomach reminding me of how little I'd eaten since I'd left my lands more than a day ago. I approached the campsite with caution, aware of the potential danger of the situation.

We approached the campsite slowly, remaining out of sight. Three males sat around a bonfire, a deer carcass cooking above the flames. They seemed oblivious to my presence, chatting amongst themselves as they drank out of bone mugs.

I watched them for a while, unsure if I should approach them or try to sneak past. Suppose they were merely travelers or merchants moving from one town to the next. In that case, they may have made good company, providing safety in numbers while I slept, as well as more ideas to help me find my mate. From the appearance of the males, I couldn't tell whether they were merchants or bandits, but from their conversation, which mainly focused on the length of their journey and the family they hoped to return to, I had little doubt they were closely related. I was torn between the potential benefits of joining their camp and the risks of revealing myself.

Three horses were anchored on a nearby tree, seemingly at peace as they ate from the grasses of the forest floor. The group had no carts, no slaves, only meager packs and simple weapons, at least from what I could see. If they were looking for someone to rob, I held very little of value. Aside from my horse and the handful of coins in my bag, stealing from me would have been more trouble than it was worth.

If it came to it, however, having been trained by a weapons master since I was a young boy, there was a chance I could defend myself against three adversaries, but I would rather not be put in that situation at all. Still, when weighing the risks versus rewards, it was a better idea to approach the males and see what they knew, instead of moving on and hoping they didn't notice my retreat. Not only could they have seen those who'd taken my mate, but joining their camp also had the possibility of giving me a chance to rest in safety for a few hours before continuing my journey.

The forest quieted as I dismounted and walked Shadow toward the fire, increasing the sound of my footsteps so I wouldn't surprise the group. As I got closer, I lifted my hands in front of myself to show I had no weapons, clearing my throat. The heads of all three males twisted in my direction, two of them reaching for their swords as they rose to their feet. The other male, from what I could tell, was much older. Most of his hair was long gone, but what remained was stark white against his bronzed skin. Their father, maybe. The two standing males, who appeared to be around my age, looked like brothers.

"Who's out there?" One of them took a step forward, narrowing his eyes in my direction.

My steps ceasing, I dipped my head in greeting. "My name is Blaze Vathyra. I was passing through when I caught the scent of your fire, but I can move on if you would prefer. I have nothing to trade, and I don't want any trouble, just a place to rest. If the three of you would like one more sword hand in your party for protection, I could travel with you for a time."

Keeping my hands where they could see them, I attached Shadow's reins to a nearby tree and took another few steps forward.

"Are you alone?" The same male who'd spoken before, the older of the two brothers, with long, black hair and equally dark eyes, scanned the surrounding forest for more intruders. Seeming to sense none, he returned his sword to its scabbard and sat back down on the log near the others.

I continued my steady approach, keeping my hands as far away from my sword as I could, trying to not appear as a threat. "I came alone, which we could agree puts me at more risk than you."

When I said the final few words with a disarming grin, the one I suspected was the father dipped his chin in acceptance, and the three males seemed to appreciate my candor. Relief filling me just as much as my exhaustion, I lowered myself onto a log near the fire, reveling in the warmth it provided.

"My name is Cailean Oathorne. This is my older brother Fionn, and my father is Baltair," the youngest male said as he poked at the fire with a stick, sending embers twirling into the air. "Where are you headed?"

Hoping the family was trustworthy, I provided an explanation of where I'd been and where I was going, even sharing with them about my mate, how she'd been taken from the portal shortly after she arrived in our world.

Three horrified faces looked back at me as I explained, but they didn't appear surprised. Baltair scratched at the scruff on his chin, glancing at his two sons before he spoke. "Their mother came from the human lands many decades ago. If it hadn't been for my key, I would have spent my entire life as a very lonely man, would probably be only ash by now, with no sons to carry on our family name and its legacy. Anything we can do to help you find your female. We'll do it. If we can."

My heart swelled with the older male's admission and his offer. "Where is your mate now? Is she still in this realm?" I knew she couldn't have returned to the human realm, but I didn't want to ask the male if his wife was still alive.

Baltair nodded, a grin tugging on the side of his mouth. "Oh, yes. My sweet Alice is back home, tending to the grandchildren and Fionn's mate while we go to the capital of the Court of Knowledge in search of a healing potion for my youngest grandson. The healers could not cure his illness, but rumors claim there is a special potion at the Tower of Healing in Cloudfell." The pain that crossed the face of the oldest brother made it clear the ill child was his own.

Among fae, it was still unusual, even after decades of the key system, for a human to build a life here without vanishing into a noble's household. Baltair spoke of it as if it were the most ordinary thing. Still, the way his sons glanced at each other told me they'd grown up in a household marked by whispers and sideways looks from their neighbors.

I'd only heard of the Tower of Healing in rumors—its green-glass spire catching sunlight over the Ink Quarter of Cloudfell, its halls lined with scrolls older than the four Courts themselves. Some said the priests there could draw sickness out of a body and seal it in crystal jars; others said they only hoarded remedies for the rich.

I turned my eyes back to Baltair. "I'm sorry to hear of the child's illness and hope you're able to find a cure. Where are you traveling from? "

Cailean answered, still poking at the fire. "We come

all the way from the Court of Courage. We've been traveling for weeks."

Familiar with the Court of Courage's location, I didn't envy the males for having to travel such a distance. It was indeed a long trip.

"You shouldn't have much further to go, right? I've never been to the capital city of Cloudfell, but I would hope we're not more than a few days' ride from there."

The father nodded, stretching his arms above his head as he yawned. "We were just discussing the same thing when you came upon us. We travel by night and rest during the day. It's too dangerous to linger in these woods after dark." He arched a bushy white eyebrow at me. "I'd imagine that was your plan as well?"

I nodded, my own exhaustion growing as I sat in front of the fire. "I've been traveling since yesterday morning. I made it to the Sanctuary of Healing last night and met with the Healer on High. After she told me what happened, she and I traveled to the portal together to look for clues, but there were none. There was nothing but an empty cave. No human females. No guards. I left her a short time later and traveled toward the Court of Knowledge first, since it was closest to the portal. It was Tansey's assumption that they couldn't have taken my mate very far, since all the human women who cross the portal are very sick. Most of them need healing as soon as possible if they're going to survive, which is why they all pass through the Sanctuary to be treated before joining their mates. Wherever they took her, she can't be far... At least not until she's well enough to travel."

A knowing grimace flashed across Baltair's face. "Then you must find her soon, before she's auctioned off to someone in a faraway kingdom, and it's too late."

I knew it was true, but hearing it out of someone else's mouth only made the tightness in my chest that much stronger. There was no time to waste. I had to find her. "That's my fear as well. It's why I haven't stopped to rest, or even eat, since I left the Sanctuary."

Even though my mind knew time was of the essence, my limbs were weighed down with fatigue as I sat by the fire, the added safety of having company giving my body the permission it needed to relax. If only I could close my eyes for a moment, then I could ride through the night and hopefully find the first brothel by the next day.

Noticing his father's exhaustion, Cailean rose, pulling a tent from one of their packs and erecting it only a few paces away. Fionn stood to help his brother.

Once his sons finished setting up their shelter, Baltair headed toward his tent, placing his hand on my shoulder as he passed. "If you have a tent, my suggestion is to use it. Get a few hours of sleep. We'll set off again before nightfall. If you're looking for brothels or auction houses where she may be kept, I would imagine we'll pass some on our way to the capital. You're welcome to continue traveling with our company. There's safety in numbers, after all."

I had packed little, but I had brought a tent. I knew my mate would need rest as we journeyed back to my lands, and although I'd intended to stay at inns with her, I'd brought one just in case.

The decision to set up my own tent near the others was made more out of exhaustion than out of confidence in my safety. There were obvious dangers to letting my guard down in the forest, just like there were potential risks in trusting Baltair and his sons, but I needed rest. Even with the risks, my instincts told me that the males were who they said they were, and I'd much rather rest near others, and near a fire, than rest somewhere in the dangerous forest by myself. With no energy left, I swallowed my doubt and stepped into the small tent, sliding beneath the blanket with my clothing and boots still on, my weapons only inches from my hand.

Thoughts of her, whoever she was, swirled through my mind as I tried to clear it for sleep. I thought about what she was like. What color was her hair? Her eyes? Would her eyes light up when she looked at me? I wondered if she understood how the key worked, how it made us destined for each other, or if she would deny me.

Just the thought of her turning me away threatened

to rip my heart into pieces, but I forced those worries away. We were meant to be together, our keys intertwining our destinies as though we had been born for each other. She may not love me right away, but I planned to work every day for the rest of my life to make sure I was everything she could ever want. Something beautiful would bloom between us, something forever. *If* I could find her.

Somewhere in the fantasies of a life with my female in it, my mind became too drained to stay conscious any longer. I drifted off to sleep, visions of my perfect mate keeping me company until the darkness pulled me under.

CHAPTER SIX

Elianna

When I woke up the next morning, my first morning in the human quarters, the shared space was alive with activity, making it nearly impossible to dwell in my own thoughts and fears. Zoe was already gone, the other bed in the room empty and made, but the sounds of women in the next room were hard to miss. Pulling on one of the light blue shift dresses left hanging on a hook by the door, I slipped my feet into my slippers and entered the chaos of the main living area.

No less than nine women flitted about the space, most of them either eating from the spread of breakfast on the large table on one side of the room or lounging on the other. I scanned the space looking for my roommate, but of all the women in and around the space, Zoe wasn't one of them. I knew my new friend was forced to work in the brothel, but the thought of it still made my stomach churn. It wasn't a life I was used to back in the human realm, not that anyone could ever get used to women being forced into sexual servitude. I wondered if that was where Zoe was at that moment, wondered if that was where all twelve of the other human women were. The growing uneasiness in my stomach settled only slightly when the bathroom door opened, and the familiar head of blond hair walked out.

Zoe smiled as she moved toward the pastries waiting on the table, lowering herself into one chair and grabbing a muffin. "Good morning, Elianna. How'd you sleep?"

I shrugged, the rumble of my stomach overtaking the stress-induced nausea. I reached for a scone, dropping into the chair next to Zoe. "As well as I could sleep in my present situation. It didn't take me as long to realize where I was when I woke up today versus yesterday. I'm not sure that's exactly a good thing." Shifting uncomfortably in my chair, I took a bite of the berry pastry, but it tasted like sand in my mouth. I poured myself and Zoe a cup of tea. "Do you have to... um... to work today?" I knew it wasn't a job at all, not for the women in Lord Argall's control, but I didn't know how else to phrase it. Zoe was being forced to allow males to use her body, and she wasn't getting paid. It wasn't a job. It was slavery. *Abuse.*

Grimacing, Zoe's eyes revealed more than she'd probably intended. I hadn't known the blond for more than a day, but I recognized a woman who did her best to appear tougher than she really was. Or she was tougher than she appeared. Not knowing what ailment had forced my new friend to make the tough choice to leave her world, I figured it was the latter. We were all tougher than we appeared, every single one of us.

One of the other females, a brunette a little older than me, pulled out a chair across the table and sat. "We both do," she said, reaching out to touch my hand. "I'm Lauren. I missed your arrival last night."

Taking Lauren's hand, I smiled. "I'm Elianna. How long have you been here?"

Pouring herself a cup of tea, Lauren reached for a buttered roll and took a bite. "Hard to say. The fae don't keep time like we do. Maybe a few months."

"Do you think your mate is still looking for you?"

Lauren bristled at my question, her smile faltering for a moment. "I'd like to think so, but I admit I've lost hope for that. After a while, I wondered if he even existed, if being with a destined mate was my purpose here at all. Maybe the claims of a companion waiting for us were only a trick, a ploy meant to sway us to cross the portal, only to become this, a warm hole for lonely fae males to put their cocks in."

I flinched, Lauren's blunt words hitting the hollow spot growing inside my chest, where all my doubts went to roost and fester. Zoe didn't respond, seeming to be well-versed in Lauren's brashness. "Do you ever wonder if he'll find you at the brothel? Not as a patron, but do you think he'll track you down there? I mean, these males wait for mates their entire lives. They wouldn't give up hope so quickly." I realized I was trying to make myself feel better more than I was trying to comfort my new friends.

Lauren shrugged before leaning forward on the table. "Might be a problem when our keys are locked away in a safe that blocks magic."

What Lauren had said about our keys being locked away in a chamber that blocked their magic threatened to shatter all remaining hope inside me. To my surprise, however, she knew where the safe was because she'd claimed to have serviced Lord Argall in his chambers more than once. *Serviced* him. I couldn't even pretend to not know what those words meant, but I pushed them out of my mind. Well, I tried to. I spoke with the two women for a little longer, until my new companions had to leave for the brothel, where they had to perform the duties they had all but accepted.

Returning to my bedchamber after they'd left, I dwelled in my thoughts. According to Lauren's claim, the safe in question was kept in Lord Argall's office, hidden behind a tapestry on the wall. Having no magic of her own, Lauren could not open the safe and retrieve the keys herself, but she saw the glimmer of them when he'd opened it in front of her. It was surprising that the lord revealed the safe's location in front of Lauren, but he clearly didn't see the human woman as a threat enough to hide it from her. I didn't know how I was going to get into the safe, or even how I would get into the lord's private rooms, but I knew I had to try. I just hoped I wouldn't be forced to offer my body to do so.

Hiedra returned later that morning to collect me and two other women who would perform cleaning duties in the manor. Considering the alternative, I was happy to scrub whatever I needed to, especially if it got me closer to finding the lord's private office. Trailed by one of the fae guards, a young male with fiery red hair and eyes the color of spring grass, as well as Hiedra, I had little chance to talk with the other two human women in my group. Neither of which I'd become acquainted with.

Escorted around the massive estate, I did my best to map out the property, paying attention to doors and windows, as well as any way I could get outside. We were shown into the expansive library and taught how to clean the shelves and organize the books. How anyone could have a library rivaling some I'd only seen in historic cities in the human world blew my mind. I wished I could spend time there and get lost in the ancient books and manuscripts, but I knew that would never happen.

Once leaving the library, we were brought into a study, the dining room, and four guest rooms with attached bathrooms. Every space was more im-pressive than the next. Shiny marble floors spread throughout the home, alongside the rich, dark hardwoods, which perfectly matched the book-shelves that warmed the library. There was no time for me to admire the artwork displayed on the walls, or the beautiful sculptures expertly placed through-out, not with our escorts rushing us along. Lord Argall's wealth was evident even without seeing the entire property. I hated to think how he afforded it all.

After being shown the rooms we would clean, the three of us, human women, were led into the kitchen and introduced to the cook, Wilhere. Leav-ing us in the kitchen to help prepare for dinner, Hiedra returned to her own chores, whatever they were.

Wilhere, the head cook, was an older fae male, although I realized their aging slowed enough that he could have been ancient, and I wouldn't have known. With the hunch of his back and the white of his hair, I wondered why he was still slaving in a kitchen instead of relaxing at home, enjoying a long retirement. It only took me a moment to realize he was probably just as much a slave as I was. The thought made my breakfast sour in my stomach. I hoped that, if the cook was a slave, maybe he'd at least be kind to us while we worked in the kitchens. No one had been cruel to me yet, but I would not let myself fall into a false sense of security.

Although it didn't look like the modern kitchens of the human realm, the kitchen in the manor was immense. Candles lit the square room along with sconces on the walls, throwing the corners of the room into shadow. Three wooden stoves lined the side wall, each with a large pot over its fire, steam rising as the contents cooked. A brick oven built into another wall generated heat, the scent of freshly baked bread filling the space. My stomach grumbled, and I suddenly regretted not eating much of the breakfast we'd been given that morning.

As the cook spoke to our small group, I was utterly lost in my own thoughts, the instructions Wilhere gave flying past me, bypassing my ears altogether. If there was any opportunity for me to sneak out and explore the manor, it would be when I was supposed to be working in the kitchen. I thought about it as I cut potatoes at a large prepping table. Planning my escape, no matter how far-fetched, was a way to keep my mind occupied on thoughts other than those that threatened to destroy my spirit. Hope of escape was still hope, even if it was foolish.

I was just starting on the onions when one of the other women, no older than I was, took a seat on the bench next to me, knife in hand to help with the prep work. Her smile was sweet as she looked at me, her freckles making her appear even younger than she probably was.

"I'm Jenny," the young woman said in a conspiratorial way that made me scan the kitchen for anyone listening. Thankfully, no one was paying attention. The other, who had been in our group, a twenty-something woman with obsidian hair, was on the other side of the extensive kitchen, engaged in conversation with the cook as the human washed dishes.

"My name is Elianna," I spoke in only a whisper. Just because no one appeared to be paying attention didn't mean no one was. The guard who'd escorted us around the property had been replaced by a slightly older male who'd taken up a spot near the door. He leaned with one foot braced on the wall behind him, his expression unreadable. "How long have you been here?"

Jenny pursed her lips. It seemed Lauren wasn't the only one who'd forgotten how long she'd been in the fae realm. "About three weeks. Could be longer. I'm not sure how long I was unconscious before I woke up in the infirmary."

Until that moment, I thought I'd only been asleep for a few hours, maybe a day, before I'd woken up in the stark white room. After speaking to Jenny, I was no longer sure of that timeline.

"What made you decide to cross?"

Taking in Jenny's features, I wasn't even sure if the young woman was old enough to be here. Jenny smiled, and I realized I'd been staring. "Well... I was on the heart transplant list. Congenital heart disease. Time began running out on me. I thought about it, you know." Jenny shrugged, a smile still spanning her freckled face. "I'm sure we all do. There was a good chance I would've gotten a match at the eleventh hour, but even surviving that surgery with as sick as I was, with as much as my body had started to give up on me... Let's just say I wasn't all that confident in my ability to live a full and healthy life if I stayed there."

The cook walked past us, taking the potatoes we'd cut and dropping them into one of the large pots. Jenny quieted until he was once again out of hearing range. "If I'd known I would be snatched and thrown into the role I have now, I'm not sure if I would've made the same decision. It is better than being dead, though. At least for me. At least for now."

The side of my mouth tugged up in a smile, and I nodded, but I still wasn't sure how I felt about my own choice. I knew I probably wouldn't know if I'd made the right decision until I saw what my role would be in Ecromos once my body was fully healed, until I knew if my new master would mistreat me. There was still a chance my mate could find me. It was a hope I couldn't let go of just yet, not if I was going to hold on to my will to live. My will was shaky and frayed, at best.

"What about you?" Jenny asked, but the guard shushed us before I could answer. He moved closer, leaning against the wall only a few feet from our bench.

"Cut these roots," Wilhere said as he dropped a bundle of carrots on the table in front of us. The other woman of our group left the dishes she'd just finished washing and took a seat across from us to help with the roots.

"This is Raven," Jenny said, but the guard shushed her again. The redhead rolled her green eyes but didn't talk back. The dark-haired guard was handsome, but the grimace on his face brought him from an eight to a four and made him completely unapproachable. With him looming so close by, the three of us women were forced to continue our work in silence. The only sound remaining was that of our three blades hitting the wooden table, the blades, and the thoughts swirling like a vortex in my mind.

CHAPTER SEVEN

Blaze

Shortly after sunset, the three Oathorne males and I packed up our camp and set off on horseback toward Cloudfell, the capital of the Court of Knowledge. Even with the urgency of finding the female who already held my heart, the exhaustion from my hours of travel had pulled me into several dreamless hours of sleep. Not even visions of the human female who was destined for me found their way into my subconscious mind as I lay below the blankets in the small tent. Upon waking, my companions had shared some of their roasted meat and ale with me, filling my belly for the long journey ahead.

We kept our conversations light as we traveled through the forest, speaking low enough to not be heard by other fae or by the creatures lurking in the jumble of trees and brush. I learned a bit more about my companions as we ate, including about Fionn's fae wife and children, but I'd learned very little about the youngest brother, who appeared to be the closest to my age. Slowing Shadow's pace until I was walking alongside Cailean, I pulled out my water skin and handed it to him.

"What about you, Cailean? Do you have a female?"

Taking a swig of water, the youngest brother gave the waterskin back to me as he shook his head. Fionn looked over his shoulder and shot me a grin, but didn't slow his pace or comment. "Not yet, but I have my key." Cailean shrugged, the gesture half-hearted as he patted his pocket. "It only flashed a few times, probably when it was given to my mate. I keep it with me, though, hold it in my hand often, hoping she feels me urging her to come to me. It's up to her if she chooses to cross the portal, but I'll send my hopes through it until she does, or until it—" He hesitated, running his hand down his face. I could see the longing there, tinged with a hint of sadness. "I'll send everything I have through that key—until she's here, or until it's too late."

I didn't need Cailean to explain what he meant by it being too late. It was the same fear I'd had over the weeks and months that I held my own key, making the same pleas to it. When I'd held the enchanted object in my hand, my power, love, and desires pulsing through it, I'd hoped she wouldn't choose to die instead of being with me. If only I'd had a way to see her back then, to speak with her, then I could have told her how much her life would improve if she left her realm to be with me. There was so much more than just a cure. I had been so afraid she would decide to give up on life instead. It would have killed me to see my key go dark, to know my destiny left the world without ever knowing I was there waiting for her, without ever knowing she was everything I'd ever wanted. I couldn't bear to think about the fact that she still would never know those things if I couldn't find her. The backs of my eyes burned as those worries plagued me, but I turned my attention back to the male riding beside me. I knew what Cailean was going through because I'd gone through it too.

"I remember what that was like, and you're doing the right thing. I did the same. Keep sending your affections through the key. Keep reminding her you're here waiting for her. Hopefully, it'll be enough to make her take the chance to leave her world." I cycled a deep breath, a warning I wished I'd been given waiting on my tongue. "And go to the sanctuary immediately. The minute that light flares to life and doesn't let up, go straight to the portal entrance. Whoever stole my female took her as soon as she crossed, so please don't give them the chance to steal yours, too. Be there before they can take her."

Cailean's bronzed skin blanched at my words, his dark eyes wide, as he nodded. We all knew the journey I was on. We all understood what was happening to the human females in our realm, and it needed to stop. Every male who held a key and waited for their companion to cross needed to be on alert, because all the human females were at risk of being stolen from the portal just as my mate had been. Those who came into our world came seeking healing and a fresh start, as well as love and companionship. They didn't go into the fae realm to be sold into slavery and forced to work on their backs in brothels, or in the homes of those who could afford them. It was unconscionable. That future was not better than death, not for many of them. Regardless of whether I found my mate, I intended to be part of the force that would protect the portal, as well as protect the females who crossed through it until the male with the twin key arrived. I couldn't stand by and allow more humans to be stolen. It was a vow I made to myself as Shadow's hooves landed silently on the forest floor.

Signs of a settlement came into view just as dawn approached, the hours of traversing the dense forest making my eyelids heavy. I couldn't waste another moment until I found her, but my body threatened to collapse if I didn't rest. So, when Baltair aimed his horse toward the front of a lone tavern with an attached inn, relief bloomed inside me, relief tangled with guilt. I would only sleep for a short while, a few hours, and then I would set back out, even if my new companions weren't ready to leave. It was what I thought about as Shadow kept pace behind the other three horses. If I needed to stop, I hoped I'd at least be able to talk with some locals. Perhaps someone has information that could help me find my mate, so I can bring her home. When we arrived at the tavern, I followed behind the father and his two sons, intending to do precisely that.

A roughly carved sign reading *The Laughing Tree* hung on a chain outside the door. Stacked boulders and hardwood logs comprised the rustic structure, and most of the outer walls were windowless; the lack of life felt palpable from the outside.

"As good a place as any," Baltair said as he tied up his horse to one post in the structure's front, his brown mare immediately burying her muzzle into the long grasses at her feet.

I scanned the surrounding forest before attaching Shadow's reins to another post, but it seemed to be the only building in the area. We'd passed a few cabins in the past few miles, but nothing substantial. We were still a long ride away from the city of Cloudfell.

Being in such an isolated area, and it being barely dawn, I wasn't surprised that only six people were sitting inside. Most of the patrons had probably come from the attached inn, or were traveling through, just as we were. The aroma of home-cooked food wafted through the air. Plates of eggs, porridge, and roasted meat lay before nearly every customer. My stomach rumbled, reminding me it had been hours since I'd eaten back at the fire of our last campsite.

"Busy spot," Cailean said as he shut the door behind us.

Grunting his agreement, Fionn dipped his chin toward the bar. "Grab a table. I'll check with the barkeep about renting rooms, at least for a few hours." I nodded and took a seat at one of the empty tables along the wall. Baltair and Cailean joined me.

Hardwood beams supported the upper floor, lanterns attached to them creating eerie shadows around the mounted animal heads that hung on the walls. A server approached the table as soon as we sat down, dropping off mugs of coffee and taking our order. I ordered four of the breakfast specials, which appeared to be the only meal available. I wasn't sure if my companions had much money, but it was the least I could do after the hospitality they'd shown me. Baltair and his sons had already shared their food with me, their fire, and the safety of their company as I'd traveled through the forest. I would forever be indebted to them.

Fionn returned just as the server dropped off our food, multiple room keys in his hand. Reaching for the antique key inside my pocket, I ran my thumb along the intricate design, closing my eyes. My power flowed through it, but nothing flared back. I thought of her, whoever she was, and willed the enchanted object to help me find her, but it had gone silent.

"Your key," Fionn said as he held the silver object out to me, and I pulled my hand out of my pocket to take it. "I told the barkeep that we'd only be here until midday. He said we're only a day's ride away from the outskirts of Cloudfell." No matter how badly I wanted to find my mate, my exhaustion made it difficult to think about spending more hours on my horse. "I also asked the barkeep about nearby brothels."

The word was like a blade coming off Fionn's tongue, his grimace revealing how he felt about what was happening to the human women entering our realm. It affected me the same way; thoughts of my fated partner being put in that position brought bile into my throat. "Thank you for asking." The older brother shrugged as he took a bite of his eggs. "How far away is the closest one?"

"Not until Cloudfell," Fionn responded, taking a sip of his coffee. "There's one more thing..." He hesitated as he scanned the tavern, probably to make sure no one else was paying attention to our conversation. "He mentioned an auction. In three days. An auction for females."

An auction. My blood chilled. The word, and the implications of it, was evil given a name. "Who's running the auction?" It took everything in me to keep my voice calm and low enough to remain unheard by the other patrons.

Baltair and Cailean stopped eating, paying closer attention to the conversation, Cailean undoubtedly concerned about the well-being of his own mate. She wasn't in our world yet, at least not as far as he knew, but the possibility of her being abducted as well was not lost on them.

"The auction will be held at an estate near Cloud-fell. The male sitting at the bar told me about it when he heard me asking the barkeep about a brothel." Trying to be discreet, I looked past the eldest son's shoulder. Only one person was sitting at the bar, a heavy black hooded cloak hiding his face. "That was all he said. I couldn't even get a good look at him."

The rest of our breakfast went by in a tense silence, all four of us too tired to plan our next step. I hadn't even asked whether the father and two sons would accompany me as I searched the dark underbelly of the Court of Knowledge for my mate. The Oathorne males were on their own quest, one no less urgent than my own. They needed to find the potion they hoped would cure Fionn's ailing child, and that would have to be their priority.

The bar began to fill up with the rising sun, so we left the tavern and moved to our rooms. None of us wanted anyone to know that I was looking for a stolen human female, especially not when someone in that court was running the flesh trade. Anyone in the tavern could have been involved and preferred to get rid of us rather than lose their potential profits. That, or they would move the auction location so I couldn't find it. If I were going to find my match, I couldn't let that happen. I needed to be able to move through the brothels and auctions without drawing attention to myself, no matter how disturbing it would be to be there.

Lying on the lumpy bed in the tiny room above the tavern, I thought about my missing female. No matter how exhausted I was, sleep eluded me. The silver key was heavy in my hand, the weight of my mate's circumstances making it feel like a boulder. I hadn't seen it flash since the morning she'd crossed into my world, making me wonder if her key had been taken away from her. It was a heartbreaking possibility. That key was meant for her. It was her one link to me, its pull helping me to find her. Without it, I was lost.

CHAPTER EIGHT

Elianna

To my relief, we had been given a bowl of stew and fresh bread once the food was ready and had been served to the more important people on the property. By that point, I'd been starving. It wasn't the best meal I'd ever had, but everything tasted better once I knew I wouldn't throw it up after eating.

The cancer symptoms were all gone, aside from the weight I still needed to gain, which was a revelation I had yet to comprehend fully. I'd eaten the meaty root vegetable stew and even the morning's pastry with no nausea and with no difficulty breathing. The absence of my oxygen cannula was still noticeable, like a lost limb, but walking without pulling the tank behind me was a freedom I hadn't realized I'd missed. Sure, I sometimes got caught in a moment of feeling like I was forgetting something important, but I no longer needed it. It would take time for my mind to catch up with my body. Still, if my lungs could heal this completely, then the rest of me could too. Maybe strength would come back, enough that I wouldn't just sit waiting for fate to shuffle me around like a pawn. I couldn't depend only on being found. I had to be ready to move when the chance came.

I couldn't remember the last time my body had handled the everyday functions that so many took for granted without struggle, but I wasn't complaining, at least not about that. With the guard's proximity making it nearly impossible for Jenny and me to talk, there wasn't much else for me to think about aside from my mate and the miraculous cure I'd received.

Raven had been sent to deliver the meal to Lord Argall shortly after the food had finished cooking. It was a task I was glad to have not been given, even if I wanted to find out where he kept the enchanted safe. After hearing how the owner of the property made Lauren give her body to him, I hoped to stay as far away from him as I could. My unequivocal need to steer clear of the master of the house complicated things, because I needed to find my key.

I realized it was probably a pipe dream. With me being a newcomer to the fae world, there was so much I didn't know. I had no powers, nor did I have freedom. None of the human women at the manor did. The fae, however, had abilities I could only dream of, or at least that's what I'd always been told. Their world was magical, magical enough to cure terminal illnesses. If that wasn't power, I didn't know what was. It only filled me with more trepidation at the thought of going up against Lord Argall, or any of his kind.

The manor house was so large that I had yet to cross paths with anyone who appeared to be the lord, nor had I seen his wife, who I heard was a human woman. I wondered how the lord's wife felt about her husband collecting and selling human women when she'd come to the fae world under the same circumstances, or if she was even aware. There was a chance his mate was just as much of a prisoner as we were, but we had no way to know without talking to her.

The thought unsettled me, but it also sharpened a question I hadn't dared ask myself before: if women like us could end up chained to this place, did that mean we could also find ways to unchain each other? If his mate truly lived here, maybe she wasn't only a victim. Perhaps she had her own survival secrets. If so, I needed to learn them.

After lunch, Hiedra returned to the kitchens so she could escort us to the ballroom to clean one of the many rooms we'd yet to see. Raven hadn't yet returned from bringing Lord Argall his meal, which made me incredibly uneasy about what the woman was being made to do, aside from simply delivering his food. I worried about Raven, even if I didn't know her. There was a chance the dark-haired woman had returned to our quarters, but there was no way for me to know when my questions posed to our escort went unanswered. Wherever the other woman had gone, Hiedra's usual saccharine smile had soured, and it was clear the servant had no intention of explaining the missing woman's whereabouts.

We had been given little information as we followed behind the guard and the gossamer-winged servant.

All we'd been told was that a party would be held at the manor two days later, the reason for the celebration unknown to me. I walked close to Jenny. With Zoe at the brothel, the red-headed young woman was my only companion, at least for the day. My biggest fear was that I would be auctioned off the night of the party, which filled me with dread as I swept floors and waxed surfaces. Jenny had been there for weeks and had not yet been sent away, so all I could do was hope I would be kept in Lord Argall's custody long enough to find my key. When I left my key behind, I was afraid I could never be found by my mate.

Out of all the things that caused me worry, I knew being found by my mate was the most important thing in my life at that moment. He could bring me safety and could bring about the end of my captivity. I didn't know who my mate was, but something in my heart told me that, whoever he was, he would be better for me than what I would face in Lord Argall's control. That was the only hope I had, the only thing keeping me from spiraling into the depths of despair and regret. Even if the person who bought me at the auction treated me well, I would still have been purchased, and that didn't sit right with me. Even though I knew the males in Ecromos were desperate for mates, for companions and children, it didn't ease my feelings about being sold like nothing more than a common household item, because with the purchase of me, I would still be a slave.

I knew little about the enchanted keys, but the romantic part of me wanted to believe that the twin of my key belonged to my soulmate, to the male who was meant to be mine forever. When I went to bed that night, choosing to go to sleep early after the exhausting day, it was he whom I dreamed about. Even if I didn't know his face, my mind created one for me, and with that, the fantasy of a life we could have together bloomed in my dreams, painting a future I knew I couldn't live without.

Morning came too early for me. Thoughts of a life with my mate still playing like a movie through my mind as I slept, but I couldn't ignore the shuffling of my bed, not when someone was clearly trying to wake me. Moaning, I rolled over and rubbed the sleep from my eyes when I noticed a larger set of eyes, almond-shaped and dark green, peering back at me.

The creature, only about two feet tall, peered up at me under a filthy, pointy brown hat that flopped over as though it had given up on life. With tanned, wrinkled skin and exaggerated features, the creature resembled a tiny, old man, one with enormous, pointy ears. Long tufts of brown hair shot out from beneath his hat at unnatural angles, making it appear stiff and straw-like. Two bony hands with gnarled fingers held on to my blanket as though it was preparing to yank it right off me.

Gasping and shoving away from the figure, I blinked rapidly, unsure if I was really seeing what I thought I was seeing. Maybe I was still dreaming? It only took a moment for me to realize I couldn't have been dreaming, because my imagination wasn't wild enough to conjure up such a creature. Before I processed the scene in front of me, the miniature being stopped trying to make my bed with me in it and pulled its hands away with an agitated huff.

"Well, I can't do my chores very well with you lying like a lazy pile of bones in the bed," it said in a high-strung, high-pitched, clearly disgruntled voice. I blinked again, shaking my head as I looked at Zoe's bed, hoping my friend could explain what was happening. Aside from the little creature in front of me, the bedroom was empty. "I can't stand around here all day, Missy. I have other chores, you know." He yanked on my blanket again, nearly hard enough to pull me onto the floor.

Still confused, I stood, moving to the side, so the tiny figure, dressed in a colorless burlap sack with holes for its arms and head, could finish its work. "Forgive me, but who are you? I wasn't aware that it was someone else's chore to make my bed."

The exasperated look the tiny creature gave me was like the one my grandmother used to make when my cousins and I would get into mischief. "Clean all the beds and no one notices." The tiny male seemed to no longer be speaking to me but was instead talking to himself as he leaned over to tuck my sheets beneath the mattress. "Does anyone ever notice all Pith's hard work? No, they do not. Talk over Pith. Ignore Pith. Never tell Pith hello or ask him about his day."

Although I still didn't know what kind of creature he was, Pith, I assumed was his name, had moved on to fluffing my pillows as he shook his head and continued to mumble to himself. I stood back and watched, completely beside myself. I'd never seen a creature like him.

Just as I was about to apologize to the little guy, the door cracked open and Zoe's blond head popped in. "Pith," Zoe said, as though scolding a naughty dog, "I told you not to wake her up."

Shooting the other woman an insolent look, Pith snapped his fingers and vanished from where he stood. My eyes grew wide as I stared at the space that had not been empty only moments before.

"Sorry," Zoe said as she walked into the room and shut the door behind her. "I told that little shit to let you sleep because you needed your rest, but he listens about as well as a brick in the wall."

"What was that thing?" Grabbing a clean dress from the hook near the door, I waited for my friend to answer.

"Don't wear that today. Wear this instead." Pulling two tunics and trousers from a drawer, Zoe handed me a set before she started getting dressed. "Pith is a brownie, one of a few who work in the manor. They clean, supposedly love it, but they do more grumbling than anything else. I'm not even sure why Lord Argall keeps them around. Their attitudes could use some work."

I had never heard of such a creature before, but Zoe's assessment of Pith's attitude was spot on. "Are there many creatures like Pith in this realm?"

Slipping her feet into a pair of black boots, Zoe shrugged. "I've only seen a couple of creatures in Ecromos that we don't have in our world so far, but I haven't ventured away from the lord's properties, so I'm sure there are more than those I've seen." Standing, Zoe handed me a pair of boots, nudging me to get ready. I was still unsure what our day would entail, but I obliged. "I've seen plenty of brownies, though. There are three of them here at the manor, and there are two at the brothel. They come and go as they please, never using the door like normal people, so you don't really know when they're going to pop in on you and bless you with their sunny personalities." Zoe's eye roll was hard to miss, making me snicker. "You'll see Pith the most. He's the one who comes into our rooms to straighten up. I'm not even convinced if it's really part of his duties, or if he just likes to come in here because he enjoys having someone to complain to. There are usually a few warm bodies in our rooms to listen to him."

After tying the laces on my boots, I stood back up to face my friend. "So, why are we dressing like this today?"

Zoe grinned as she opened the door. "It's a surprise."

CHAPTER NINE

Blaze

As I contemplated my friend and the key in my hand, exhaustion overwhelmed me, and I fell into a deep sleep devoid of dreams and fantasies about the life I hoped to have once I found her. When I finally awoke, the sun had already crossed the sky, indicating that I had slept longer than I had intended. Although I knew I needed the rest, I felt angry at myself for wasting precious time when I should have been searching for my female.

The inn was nearly silent. Even with the tavern below, my keen sense of hearing could detect no sounds of patrons relaxing after a long day of travel. Given the few customers there had been when we arrived, I didn't expect to see many familiar faces when I returned downstairs to eat before continuing my journey.

I was thankful that my room featured a private, though small, bathing area. I quickly washed myself and cleaned my teeth before leaving, knowing that I wouldn't have such amenities while riding my horse. By the time I entered the tavern, my stomach was rumbling, and the weight of my quest to find her pressed firmly on my shoulders. The longer I delayed, the slimmer my chances of success became.

Baltair was already downstairs when I walked into the tavern. The old man's white hair was freshly combed and still damp. A steaming mug of tea sat in front of him as he chatted with the barkeep. He smiled warmly at me as I approached the bar, his expression genuine rather than one of obligation.

"Say, Edgar, could you put on a pot of tea for my friend here and for my two sons? They'll be down soon," he requested.

The barkeep, a tree faerie, smiled and nodded, then turned to set the kettle on a small wood-burning stove.

Baltair turned on his stool as I took a seat next to him. "Fionn and Cailean were cleaning up when I left, so they should come down shortly," he said, just as the barkeep placed a steaming mug of tea and a bowl of stew in front of me. The rich aroma made me even hungrier.

"Have the three of you discussed where you plan to go from here or when you intend to leave?" I hesitated to ask, concerned about the answer. Traveling in a group felt safer, and I had come to enjoy the company of the trio, so I wasn't ready to part ways with them just yet. "I mean... Do you want to continue traveling together? I understand that we'll have to separate once we reach the city for you to search for medicine while I look for my mate, but it would be much safer."

Baltair took a sip of his tea as he looked over my shoulder, noticing the Oathorne sons approaching from the hall behind him. The older son nodded toward the corner table where we had sat earlier that morning. Understanding the cue, I grabbed my food and tea before joining my companions in the more private setting.

Both Fionn and Cailean had damp hair as they settled at the table. Fionn waved toward the bartender to get his attention. It only took a moment for Edgar to drop two more mugs of tea and bowls of stew on the table. I dug into my food, still waiting to hear whether I would be setting off into the forest alone. Baltair's sons had come out just as he was about to answer my question, and I didn't want to ask again.

The stew was delicious, better than I had expected in such an isolated location that received so few guests. The chunks of dark meat practically melted in my mouth, and the gravy was an herbal blend, not unlike what my mother used to make. I thought about her for a moment, the familiar taste bringing back memories of working in the fields every day, even though I didn't have to. My time spent on the farm and the weapons lessons I had with my father left me with fond memories. I missed my parents and hadn't seen them in a long while—only a few times since I got back from the war against the Court of Chaos over ten years ago.

My parents were still alive, but I hadn't found the time to return home as often as I would have liked. Once I found my mate, I would have to take her to meet them and show her how serene life in the Court of Harmony could be.

When I looked back up from my bowl of stew, I noticed Baltair was watching me. I hadn't even realized he was speaking.

"You seem to be lost in thought, my friend," Baltair said with a grin.

"I was," I replied. "Just thinking about going back home when this is all over, once I finally have her with me." From the knowing glint in his eye, I could tell that the father missed his home as well.

"I was asking if you're ready to set out again soon. My sons and I would like to keep moving toward Cloudfell. We can make it there by morning if we leave soon."

Wiping my mouth with a napkin, I nodded, feeling a sense of relief at not having to navigate the dangerous forest alone. "I'm ready now."

The four of us set off shortly after finishing our meal. The fresh scent of pine filled the crisp air as the sun dipped below the tree canopy. There had been fewer than ten patrons at the bar when we left—nine, to be exact, including the four of us. I wondered how the owner managed to stay open with so little business, but figured it was more out of passion than necessity. Although exhaustion weighed me down—my nap had been far too short—I felt relieved to be back on Shadow's back and searching for my mate.

As we moved through the forest at a near-silent pace, I kept my eyes and ears alert for any danger. A group of four posed a bigger threat than a lone rider, but that didn't mean there weren't those hidden among the trees who might attempt to attack us, especially if they thought there was profit to be had. The only sounds that reached my gifted fae ears were the chirping of birds and the occasional rustling of a rodent scurrying across the forest floor, at least for the first few hours.

Without my keen sense of hearing, I would have likely missed it—the sound of boots creeping just yards away, an attempt to sneak up on our group as we made our way down the path.

A low whistle, barely escaping my lips, caught Fionn's attention. As his horse's steps slowed, the older brother turned toward me, his dark eyes scanning the trees. I had already looked in my peripheral vision but had seen nothing. Whoever was following us had managed to stay hidden and had succeeded thus far. Still, I was sure of what I'd heard: the footsteps closing in behind us belonged to a person, not an animal. We were being followed.

Fionn nodded, carefully drawing his sword from its scabbard. He let out his own whistled chirp—a signal his father and younger brother must have recognized, as they moved to free their own weapons as if on command. Cailean released his horse's reins, pulled an arrow from his quiver, and notched it. The four of us scanned the surrounding trees for movement, the steps of our mounts falling silent as they slowed to keep their riders steady. My heart pounded as I took a breath, adrenaline coursing through me with the rush of danger.

The first male, clad in a black hooded cloak that camouflaged him in the brush, stepped into the path about a hundred yards ahead. In the dim light of the forest, the arrow directed at us was nearly invisible. I recognized the threat instantly and dug my heels into Shadow's side, who sprinted forward in an instant. "Go!"

There was no hesitation. Along with the Oathorne males beside me, I darted through the forest, our paths weaving like a maze as we tried to outmaneuver the assailant's arrows. One shot past Baltair's arm, causing him to jolt aside to avoid being struck as the arrow lodged itself into the trunk of a tree. I risked a glance behind us, hoping we were gaining ground, only to see that we were being pursued by two males on horseback, the archer having mounted his horse at some point when we weren't looking.

Cailean turned in his saddle, pulling the bow taut in his hands as he aimed and fired. The arrow struck the shoulder of one of our attackers, and the man in the black cloak screamed, nearly falling from his horse. Fionn and his father fanned out, with Fionn disappearing into the forest. It was clear the Oathorne males had discussed such an event beforehand; their signals were flawlessly recognized and followed by each other. If we survived this ordeal, I had them to thank for it. Cailean fired another arrow, and it slammed into the already injured man's arm, causing him to drop his bow. A moment later, the hooded figure fell to the forest floor beside his weapon.

I pulled on Shadow's reins, and the horse yielded to the command, slowing as I led her deeper into the dense trees. Circling slowly through the brush, I jumped off the saddle and sent the animal running away from the fight. I could see the injured man on the ground. Two arrows protruded from his hunched body, but he was still alive, grunting as he tried to pull the projectiles from his flesh. Fionn had our other attacker pinned against his chest, a dagger held at the captive's throat as he dragged the man toward where I stood next to the injured one.

Hissing through clenched teeth, blood gushed from the wound on the injured man's shoulder as I leveled the blade of my sword at his neck. Their companion flailed against Fionn, and the dagger nicked his flesh.

"What's this about?" I demanded from the attacker in Fionn's hold. The injured man on the ground was bleeding freely from his wounds and too hurt to reason with. "Who sent you?"

"We aren't telling you anything!" the captive replied, his voice resolute as he struggled to get free. Baltair and Cailean approached from the darkness, standing near Fionn with their weapons at the ready. In a movement more fluid than it should have been, Fionn's dagger jerked from the male's throat, slicing into his shoulder before returning to its previous position. Blood poured from the wound, trailing down the captive's arm and dripping onto the forest floor.

My sword still hovered over the crumpled man's neck as I spoke again. "Your friend's head will fall from his neck if you don't tell us who sent you to attack us. It would only take a slip of my hand." My voice was calm as I threatened death, even though I felt more fear than I let on. I had been to war and killed, but I had never enjoyed taking a life, especially when I didn't know their motives.

Spitting on the ground in front of him, Fionn's captive threw his body back, trying to knock the oldest Oathorne brother off him. Fionn's dagger flew again, slicing the male's other arm with a quick movement. The captive growled and went still as both of his arms leaked blood all over his pants. I lifted my weapon, the blade poised to follow through with my promise, when the man on the ground turned to look at me, his face etched in pain.

"The auction," the injured male groaned, his voice

shaking. "We know you're looking for a human girl. We couldn't let you find her."

My heart dropped like lead into my stomach. Someone had sent assassins to stop me from finding my mate. If I didn't kill them, they would report that I was still alive, and I didn't want more assassins sent after me. So, when Fionn's and my blades made their final slashes, there was no hesitation. I couldn't allow them to live, not when her future was at stake.

CHAPTER TEN

Elianna

I was certain I should have been wary of any surprises Zoe had in store, but when the blond woman took me by the hand and yanked me out of the room, I realized I had no choice but to follow. There were very few women out in the main living quarters that morning; most were probably still asleep or already at the brothel. I tried not to dwell on it as my friend pulled me to the table and sat down to fix herself a plate of porridge.

"Eat up, Elianna. We're going outside today!"

My heart leaped in my chest as I dropped into the chair next to her. I grabbed my own bowl and filled it with the unappetizing slop that constituted our breakfast. "Outside?"

Zoe nodded, a grin tugging at the corners of her mouth as she took a bite of her porridge. Excitement lit up her big blue eyes, a glimmer I hadn't seen before. Whatever awaited us outside was clearly something she looked forward to. "You and I are on gardening duty today. The lord wants to make sure the courtyard is in tip-top shape before the party tomorrow."

Holding back a grimace, I forced down another bite of my breakfast. The porridge truly had no taste, and its texture felt like slime against my tongue. It took everything in me not to gag. Perhaps it was the thought of physical labor that churned my stomach. I had never been fond of yard work, not that my condition ever truly gave me a choice. "And you like gardening because...?"

The look on Zoe's face made it clear I was missing the entire point. "A. Anything to get out of the house. Right? B. It gets us out of here." Zoe poured hot water into two mugs, dropped a tea bag into each, and slid one across the table to me. "Plus, the gardens are beautiful."

Just as I was about to ask Zoe more about it, the sound of the main suite's door flew open, slamming against the wall. We both turned in unison, and I nearly knocked my tea over as I spun in my chair to see Raven, barely conscious, being hauled in by two guards, who were lifting her by the shoulders between them.

"What the hell did you all do to her?" Zoe jumped out of her chair and dashed forward, but another guard slid in behind the others to cut her off.

"Stay right there, female. Which is her bedchamber?" He held his sword in front of him, the blade aimed at Zoe's stomach. She halted in her tracks and pointed to the room behind her, her scowl expressing more than her words could say. Raven's feet barely touched the ground as they dragged her past. The two guards unceremoniously dumped her on a bed in the room before leaving through the door they had entered. Hiedra scurried past them just as they were about to shut the door.

The moment the guards were out of the room, Zoe rushed toward the bedroom, arriving at Raven's bedside before Hiedra. I followed closely behind my friend, my heart pounding in my chest. I had felt uneasy about what happened to Raven ever since the dark-haired woman had left to take Lord Argall his lunch the day before. Now, less than a day later, she had been viciously beaten. My fear intensified at the sight of Raven's bruised face and bleeding lip. Her right eye was swollen shut, but the other opened to look at us before rolling back in her head, allowing unconsciousness to offer her relief from the pain. It was too difficult to watch, so I looked away. Whatever Raven had suffered could have happened to any of us at any moment. That was the one certainty I had, and it was something I needed to prevent, even if I didn't know how to do so.

"What did they do to her, Hiedra?" Zoe's voice rose just below a scream as she leaned over the injured woman, trying to smooth Raven's inky black hair away from her battered face.

"Oh, Miss Zoe, you know it's best if we don't discuss such things." Hiedra spoke in a placating and passive manner, and I knew my friend wouldn't accept that answer before she even spat out her reply.

"Save it, Hiedra! Who did this to her?" I, too, wanted to know the same thing, hoping that understanding could help me prevent it from happening to others—perhaps even to myself.

With her eyes still closed, Raven moaned as the servant used a wet rag to clean some of the blood from her hair. "It's best if you and Miss Elianna attend to your garden duties, Miss Zoe. Lord Argall would be most displeased if he saw you lingering when there was work to do."

A low growl escaped Zoe's throat as she leaned over Raven again, covering her friend with a blanket. "I will tend to my chores as soon as you tell me what she did to deserve this. Tell me who did this to her, and we'll leave."

When the elderly winged woman looked up to meet Zoe's gaze, her eyes were soft as she spoke barely above a whisper. "Miss Raven knew better than to disobey her master. She tried to run, and this is what happened. I suggest all the human females learn a lesson from this, since she didn't heed the warning from what happened to Miss Rebecca."

The warning left a hollow feeling in my chest, as the hope of one day escaping was ripped away from me like a rug pulled from beneath my feet. Something in Zoe snapped; her expression twisted into pure fury, her eyes locking onto Hiedra's with intensity. Her words came out slowly, saturated with venom, making me hang on every syllable. "Don't you ever say Rebecca's name again."

After that, we left the room, and I trailed behind Zoe as the guard escorted us down the hall and out the double doors into the garden. I could practically see the steam rising from my friend as she walked, her anger powering her steps, but I didn't dare speak to her. I hadn't forgotten how the guards in the kitchens silenced us whenever we tried to communicate the day before.

Once we reached the gardens, with only a few guards out of earshot, I hesitated before speaking. My voice was barely a whisper as I addressed Zoe, who had crouched near a planter bed, pulling weeds.

"Zoe? What was that all about? Who's Rebecca?"

Zoe scanned the garden before meeting my eyes. Surrounded by lush flowers and foliage, we were mostly hidden as we worked. "She was my friend."

Shaking her head slowly, Zoe tossed the weeds onto the ground and dropped to sit on her bottom, burying her face in her dirty hands. I didn't respond immediately, allowing her the moment she clearly needed. When Zoe's shoulders began to shake, I sat down beside her and wrapped my arm around her back. "What happened to her?"

Zoe didn't answer right away; her muffled cries spoke volumes. When she finally managed to respond, her words were barely a whisper. "She's dead."

Even though they were barely audible, Zoe's words hit me like iron spikes in my stomach. Women came to Ecromos seeking healing. If Rebecca were dead, it likely wasn't due to what had sent her through the portal in the first place—not with the fae healers possessing the power to bring human women back from the brink of death. I didn't respond; I didn't know any words that could ease my friend's broken heart. Someone Zoe cared about was gone, and Hiedra suggested it should serve as a warning for us all. All I could think about was the kind of warning the servant meant.

"It was earlier this year," Zoe began, her voice still low enough not to be heard by the guards. I peeked around the shrubbery, but the young guard closest to us seemed to be sleeping while standing. He didn't know we were even there. "About three months ago. We worked in the brothel together... on the same shift, I mean. Rebecca had a harder time with it. Not that any of us have an easy time. I don't mean the women who work there willingly, either. I respect the hell out of those women. But among those of us who are forced, none of us sleeps well at night. Some of us have just found ways to numb ourselves when we're there, to separate our minds from our bodies." She took a shuddering breath, a sob escaping her as she wiped her damp cheek with her sleeve. "One of Lord Argall's friends from the Court of Courage requested her to be sent to his rooms in the manor while he was here for diplomatic matters. She was so beautiful. It wasn't unusual for her to be requested." Zoe's face fell back into her hands as she tried to muffle her crying. I glanced at the nearest guard again, but he was looking in the other direction as another group of women planted new blooms.

"What happened to her?" I asked, squeezing my friend against my chest and tucking Zoe's head into my shoulder. I felt her shoulders slump.

"She never left that suite."

I felt as if my heart had been ripped from my body and torn apart. A woman had died in the manor at the hands of a fae male who intended to use her body. It was my worst nightmare, the very thing I feared most when I had debated using the enchanted key to find a cure for the incurable. I was speechless. There were no words I could say to change any of it. So, instead of asking questions or offering condolences, I let Zoe cry on my shoulder. All we could offer each other in that moment was the one thing we both needed the most: someone to be there for us when we crumbled.

The sound of boots against gravel abruptly ended our moment. Just over the bushes, I saw a guard sauntering in our direction. Zoe returned to pulling weeds, and I followed her lead as he turned the corner around the flowerbed we were working on. He continued walking by, seemingly oblivious to the hard work of the women he was supposed to be watching. I let out a relieved breath as he passed, my heart racing chaotically in my chest.

Aside from avoiding any attempts to escape and staying far away from males who wanted to use me for sex, I didn't know what else to do with the information Zoe had given me. I felt trapped. My only hope was that my mate would show up to rescue me. Like a damsel in distress, a role I had never envisioned for myself, I was as confined as an animal in a cage.

As I pulled weeds from the flowerbed, I thought about the walls of my cage with every movement of my hands. The only sound I focused on was my breathing. I knew the garden was beautiful—the scent of the flowers filled my nose—but I concentrated entirely on my task, the numbness of my emotions turning my actions robotic. I was so focused on the dirt beneath my fingers that I didn't notice Hiedra approach from behind until she cleared her throat.

Startled, I jerked back onto my heels and looked up to see Hiedra blocking the sunlight. The shadow made her lilac skin appear darker than it did in the light. Zoe didn't speak; she remained silent, watching Hiedra for a moment. The usually sweet smile on Hiedra's face was replaced with something more reserved.

"You'll need to go inside and get cleaned up, Miss Elianna," she said, her voice devoid of emotion as she looked down at us with her depthless onyx eyes. "The Master wants you to dine with him tonight. He wishes to meet his new ward."

CHAPTER ELEVEN

Blaze

When my three companions and I left the site of the attack, my sword cleaned from a nearby stream, I knew someone was aware I was searching for my mate and was willing to kill to stop me. I hoped the two males we had disposed of were the only ones who knew about my plan to attend the auction to find her, but I couldn't be sure. Either way, I needed to be cautious. Their actions reinforced my suspicions that she was in the city of Cloudfell and could be sold at the upcoming auction. If my mate hadn't been one of the women there, I doubted they would have gone through so much trouble to eliminate me.

We buried the two males who attacked us and erased any trace of the conflict. If anyone realized we had survived, more assassins would surely follow. With the slavers believing I was dead, I had been given a clean slate, effectively becoming a non-issue. If they thought my body was decomposing somewhere in the forest, no one would expect me to appear at the auction.

We had barely spoken about my plans while we were in the tavern; secrecy was vital for the element of surprise. Yet, we had still been overheard and followed. Someone involved in the flesh trade of human women had taken enough of an interest to order our murders.

As I scanned the surrounding forest from the saddle of my horse, a thought struck me. The tavern we had stopped at had very little business, and I had wondered how the owner could afford to keep it open. It occurred to me that there might be a connection between the bar owner and the attack on our lives. Although the male had been friendly, he might have been involved in the trade of stolen human women. Perhaps those who took the women from the portal provided the tavern with some of its only business, lining the owner's pockets to keep quiet. The thought made me sick and churned my stomach. While I didn't have time to uncover the truth about the tavern at that moment, I hoped to do so once I had my mate safely in my arms.

The four of us moved in relative silence. Traveling stealthily had become essential. As we approached Cloudfell, the road evened out, and the trees parted enough to allow movement by foot, horse, or carriage. With the capital of the Court of Knowledge being a hub for commerce and the arts, it attracted visitors from across the realm.

The moon was still out as we rode through the dense forest in the final hours of our journey, its light helping us travel unnoticed. Once we were only a few miles from the city center, we veered further into the trees to set up a makeshift camp.

We needed to eat, rest, and plan our next moves away from prying eyes.

Fionn rode his horse deeper into the forest to scan the area for other encampments or travelers while the rest of us set up camp. I started a small fire, and Cailean went out hunting, his skill with a bow a valuable asset for securing food. I could hunt as well, but it wasn't my strongest skill.

Baltair sat near the fire, warming his hands. The older man appeared exhausted from our journey, but his love for his sons and grandchildren was evident. I admired him for joining them on such a dangerous trek. The Oathorne males operated seamlessly as a team, and I considered myself fortunate to have met them. I knew they would be lifelong friends once our shared journey came to an end.

Once we got into the city, we would need to go our separate ways. I had to search the seedier parts of the Court of Knowledge to find my mate. At the same time, the Oathorne males needed to look for the tonic that would help Fionn's ill son—if such a miracle potion even existed. I still knew little about the child's condition, and the need for quiet travel had prevented long conversations. I also felt it was inappropriate to bring up such a sensitive topic anyway.

When Cailean returned, he had a large rabbit in his hand. I had already brewed tea, and the fire was ready to cook our meal. Fionn came back a short time later, confirming that there were no other fae nearby who might stumble upon us. As we all sat down to eat, I took the first deep breath I'd managed since leaving the tavern.

"Do you think the tavern owner was involved?" I asked the others. "I mean, in the trade. While we were there, I wondered how they could stay in business with so few patrons. There were only a few people who could have overheard our conversation about my mate. Those assassins knew exactly where we were headed, which made me question whether the barkeep might have shared our destination and my reasons for going to the capital."

When I finished speaking, Fionn was already nodding. "I thought the same thing. When the cloaked man at the bar mentioned the auction, the only other person within earshot was the barkeep. But I never saw the other man's face, thanks to his hood. He could have been one of the attackers, but it's also possible the bar owner had nothing to do with it."

"I hope that's the case," Baltair said as he stifled a yawn. "If it isn't, we might have a problem. As far as we know, the barkeep is still alive. If someone else is aware of us, they may realize we aren't dead and send others after us."

"Or worse, they could move the auction so I can't find her." The words came out like gravel from my mouth. If they moved the auction and I couldn't locate it, there was a chance I would never find my mate. I needed a plan that would get me into the manor where she might be kept, so I could stay informed if they shifted the auction. This auction was the only lead I had, so it was where I needed to start. I turned to Fionn, the only one of us who had spoken to the individual at the bar, as Cailean set up the tent for their father to rest.

"Before you ask," Fionn said just as I was about to speak, "the auction will be held on a property owned by Lord Argall. He's apparently a wealthy man who lives on the outskirts of the city and is on friendly terms with the king." Fionn smirked. "I got that information from the piece of filth I pulled from his horse before he fell on my blade."

The corner of my mouth tipped up in a grin, realizing I liked Fionn even more than I had moments before. I didn't know much about what he did for a living or his past, but I had a feeling it hadn't always been legal—unless the older brother had been a soldier before settling down. The way he wielded a weapon and skillfully killed a man spoke volumes. "I don't know where I would be if I hadn't met your family. I am forever indebted to the three of you."

Fionn nodded as he watched his father climb into their tent, the old man patting me on the shoulder as he passed. Cailean, who had gone into the tent without my realizing it, must have already fallen asleep.

"There are always dangers in these forests. You helped us as much as we helped you. My father is no longer at a stage in his life where he can fight, at least not against the kind of males we had to deal with back there." Sipping his tea, Fionn tipped his head toward my pack. "Get a few hours of rest. I'll take the first watch. When the sun comes up, you should head to the manor and find your female."

I didn't know where the lord lived or what I would do once I got there, but I took Fionn up on his offer. Draining the rest of my tea, I pulled the tent from my pack and set it up next to the other one. I checked on Shadow before climbing inside, making sure she had water and a fresh patch of grass beneath her feet.

When I lay down on my bedroll, my boots still on in case there was another attack, I sifted through the options in my mind, each one more impossible than the last. By the time I pulled the key out of my pocket, the metal dull and silent, I had come up with a plan. It had been days since it had flashed to life, signaling that my mate had entered my world. My fingers traced the intricate carvings, and my body hummed with anticipation.

The plan continued to develop in my mind as I held the silver object in my hand, the silence of it disconcerting. After resting for a few hours, I would need to find an inn and clean myself up before testing my luck at the manor. With blood still spattered on my clothing—none of it my own—I didn't have a choice. I had cleaned off as much as I could in the stream, but there was still evidence of the fight all over me. If I made the wrong impression or got turned away, I would be at the mercy of the auction. I didn't even want to think about what would happen if they moved it; if they changed the location or the day and she was sold there, I might never have another chance to find her. She could end up in a faraway court, and I would never have the opportunity for a mate again. I would only ever be given that one key, and mine was matched to hers, whoever she was.

It all came down to that moment—our futures, her life, my family name. Everything was balanced precariously on my shoulders, and the weight was immense. But it was all worth it if I found her. I would ensure she had everything she wanted and would treat her like a queen. She would know every day how special she was and how much I had prayed to Solstice for her. When my exhaustion finally won over the battle with my thoughts and I drifted off to sleep, my fated mate was the last thought on my mind.

CHAPTER TWELVE

Elianna

I heard Hiedra's words but hadn't fully processed them as the winged servant stood over me. For a moment, I delved into my own mind, searching for a way out, but found none. Zoe gasped beside me, leaning over to take my hand, which I grasped gratefully. "No."

Zoe and I uttered the word at the same time. Hiedra cocked her head to the side, confusion marking her face. "You don't seem to understand, Miss Elianna. Master Argall did not make a request. You do not have the option of refusing him." I knew the servant spoke the truth, but I couldn't comply willingly—not without voicing my objections first.

"Then I want to go with her," Zoe declared, standing up and dusting off her pants. Grasping her hand, I did the same. My friend's solid presence was reassuring, even though we were equally powerless. Over Hiedra's shoulder, I caught sight of the guard approaching us, but I averted my gaze, glancing back toward Jenny and the others who were still planting flowers. I had wanted to enter Lord Argall's private quarters to look for my key, but now that the option was presented, I was shaking, terrified of meeting the same fate as Raven or Rebecca.

A churning sensation hit my stomach, forcing bile into my throat. It burned as I tried to swallow it back down. The guard stood behind Hiedra as her obsidian eyes softened. "You can't go with her to dinner, Miss Zoe, but you can join her in the bathing room. The Master expects to see you for dinner in one hour, Miss Elianna. Iain will escort you to the bathing room so you can freshen up, and Conall will come to pick you up when it's time to go. Your attire for tonight has already been brought there and is waiting for you." The servant turned to the guard, Iain, and tipped her head; the male backed up a few steps, revealing who truly held control over the situation. Looking back over her shoulder one last time, Hiedra narrowed her eyes at us. "I beg of you, Miss Elianna. Please conduct yourself in a manner befitting your best behavior tonight. The Master was quite agitated after Raven attempted to escape last night. We don't want to provoke him any further, especially not with guests arriving tomorrow. Mind your manners, be agreeable, and everything will be alright."

With that, Hiedra tipped her head back to the guard, who approached us, motioning for Zoe and me to follow him. The winged servant went in a different direction, likely returning to her chores as if nothing were wrong, as if the freedoms of other women weren't being stripped away right before her dark eyes.

We were escorted back to the bathing room where

we had initially met, and the guards stayed outside, watching the doors to prevent us from escaping—though we had no intention of trying.

There was already water in one of the large soaking tubs, and the scent of lavender filled the air. While the aroma was supposed to be relaxing, I felt anything but that as I moved toward the water and removed my filthy clothes. Working in the garden had been a sobering experience—not because I didn't enjoy the sunshine and fresh air, but because of the conversation Zoe and I had while kneeling in the grass.

I wished I had had the opportunity to speak to Jenny or some of the others before being sent off for my bath. I needed to know if they could tell me anything else about what happened to Raven, especially since I was being forced to join the lord for dinner. Hiedra claimed that Raven had been beaten because she had tried to escape after bringing the lord his food, but I knew there had to be more to the story than what had been shared with us. There had to be a way for me to escape, a way for all of us to escape. I refused to accept that there was no way out. Without hope, death was all that remained.

It was painful to think that way, to give up on all dreams of a future. Growing up in the human world, children were always encouraged to imagine what their lives would be like when they grew up. They were taught to plan their futures, to dream and plot every little step along their path. Most children don't realize all the obstacles that can stand in the way of achieving the dreams they create for themselves. Most children are never diagnosed with a terminal illness, having their futures ripped away from them before their lives even truly begin.

I knew what that was like. Crossing the portal into Ecromos was supposed to be my second chance at that future, but Lord Argall and those who kidnapped women for their own nefarious purposes had taken that from me and from all the other women in the manor house and brothel. Someone had to do something—anything—to reset the clock and give us our lives back. Even if our mates had moved on, the women who took the chance to leave their world still deserved freedom.

I thought about that freedom as I lowered myself into the steaming water, preparing my body for whatever the Master of the house had in store for me. I felt like nothing more than a slave in my own skin. Zoe washed beside me, lost in thought about something that made her eyes distant. I wondered what she was thinking about as I saw the shadows cross my friend's face, but I didn't ask. After everything I'd learned that day, especially after seeing Zoe get so upset, I knew my friend needed a moment to process her thoughts undisturbed. All I hoped was that Zoe wouldn't have to go to the brothel that night, because she had been through enough for one day. We both had.

I wasn't sure how much time had passed when Zoe turned to me, her blond hair dripping, and flashed me a regretful smile. "I've been sitting here trying to think of something to say that would convince you everything will be okay, that he wouldn't hurt you..." Zoe hesitated, glancing toward the door, where a single guard stood with his eyes averted. I appreciated his attempt to respect our modesty. With human women considered no more than objects, I hadn't expected any of the guards to refrain from gawking at our naked bodies while we bathed. "There's nothing I can say to guarantee your safety, Elianna. I don't know what happened to Raven. I don't know if he tried to touch her and she fought back, or if it was one of the guards." Zoe's voice hitched, and her eyes welled up with tears. They were already bloodshot from her crying over her late friend in the garden just hours before. "I've spent very little time with Lord Asshole. Since I'm forced to work at the brothel, I guess I'm not good enough for him. I'm not complaining, gods no. Although I don't know which is worse. Lauren has spent time with him, but she always tries to at least pretend she's accepted her fate, even if that's not how she really feels. She's the best actress I know. It's admirable. I don't know if she cries on the inside or if she cries in her bed at night, but she is one tough woman. We all are."

One shoulder lifting in a shrug, she retook my hand. It was the most I had been touched in one day since leaving my home, and I appreciated Zoe's friendship more than she probably realized. "All I can tell you is that many of the women have dinner with Lord Argall, and all have come out of those dinners in one piece, at least on the outside. Don't fight him,

Elianna. Please. Whatever you do, don't fight him. I know you still hope to see your mate one day, and I pray you get that chance, but you must survive this place for that to happen. So please, whatever you do, survive tonight."

When Zoe finished, I was speechless, my own eyes filling with tears. I didn't know how to respond to her plea for nothing more than my survival. How had the stakes in my life returned to where they had been when I was dying of cancer? I wanted more than just to survive. There had to be more to life than that for it to be worth living.

We finished washing in silence, both of us burdened with more troubling thoughts than should ever be tolerable. I hadn't known Zoe for long, but something in me told me that if my friend had the choice, she would have taken my place at dinner to preserve the hope that the newcomer had not yet lost. It broke my heart to know that. It may have only been a pipe dream, but if I ever regained my freedom, I would return for Zoe and for all of them.

After we got out of the bath and Zoe sat at a vanity to comb out her damp hair, I brushed out the tangles for her before twisting her hair into a braid. I looked at my own reflection in the mirror, my hair still so short from my cancer treatments, before looking away.

"Your hair is so beautiful," I said as I wrapped a cloth binding around the bottom of Zoe's braid. "I can't wait for mine to grow back."

Zoe smiled as she twisted in her chair. "Thank you for fixing it for me. Yours will grow back quickly. Mine was just as short as yours when I first got here. Brain tumor. The scar is just under my hairline, right here." She flipped her head to one side, parting her hair to reveal a slender two-inch scar along the side of her scalp. Rubbing absentmindedly at the scar on my throat, I felt a tightness in my chest at the sight. I had never asked Zoe what brought her here, so I was honored that my friend finally confided in me.

"They thought they got it all," she continued, her gaze drifting. "But it came back." I stayed silent as she paused, her eyes becoming distant as she glanced around the room. "When it came back the second time, I had had enough. All the treatments and surgeries, the nausea, and losing my hair—it was too much. I just couldn't do it anymore." She shrugged, her big blue eyes landing back on mine as I lowered myself onto the vanity stool beside her. "I know they probably could've opened me up again and tried to remove it, but I had the key, and it kept beckoning me. Eventually, as the medical bills piled up, I just thought, 'Forget it,' and got my friend to drive me to the Shrine. I didn't have a family to take care of me. I didn't have a husband or even a lover. Being sick was lonely, and I truly hoped that the rumors were true. I hoped I would find a soulmate here who would cure me, and then we'd live happily ever after." She let out a deep breath, chuckling softly, but I realized she wasn't genuinely laughing. "And then I woke up here."

Chills raced through my body at my friend's words. "How long ago was that?"

Zoe's blue eyes flicked up to the ceiling as if she were counting time in her head. "Close to a year, I think. They don't have regular calendars here, and it becomes hard to keep track after a while. I'm not really sure, but I don't think my mate is looking for me anymore." My already aching chest cracked at her answer, but she shrugged again, a half-hearted gesture from a woman who had learned to show toughness regardless of what she felt inside.

Suddenly, a knock sounded at the door, and a guard poked his head in; it was the same guard who had scowled at me and Jenny while we worked in the kitchens the day before. "It's time."

CHAPTER THIRTEEN

Elianna

Walking down the decorative halls to Lord Argall's private rooms felt like walking a plank over shark-infested waters. With every step, I felt myself inching closer to my doom, my heart pounding in my chest. There was no way to turn back. I kept my eyes peeled, tracking every door and window, memorizing each turn we took along the way. I knew I couldn't run; the guards stationed at every point made that impossible. Still, I mentally mapped the path, watched the guards, and tried to memorize their faces and positions. I remembered the sleeping guard in the garden. If others didn't take their jobs seriously or were too overworked to remain vigilant, then I'd have a chance.

My hands twisted in the lace and satin of my dress, a garment that felt more like a shackle than an outfit. With its low plunging neckline and a slit that rose nearly to my hip, it was much too revealing for my comfort. I had never dressed so provocatively, nor had I ever truly embraced being a girly girl. Women in the human world didn't wear clothes like this for dinners, at least not any women I knew. I was a college student—though I had taken all my classes from home, I still dressed like one and often stayed in my pajamas.

The dress was beautiful, however. Its rich cerulean color complemented my blue eyes and the warm tones of my hair, or what little I had. If Raven was the lord's type, I couldn't have been more different.

As I followed the guard, I reflected on the disturbing circumstances surrounding Lord Argall. It was hard to believe that someone of his status would engage in the trade of human slaves, especially for such purposes. Slavery had once been legal in my own world, but was outlawed long ago, recognized as the evil practice it was. I didn't know enough about Ecromos to determine if slavery was legal and sanctioned by the kings, but it seemed likely given the nobleman's affluence.

Debating the legality of my situation felt futile, especially as I was led to dinner with the man who now owned me. No other thoughts dared to invade my mind. I wondered where my mate was at that moment; the question flickered into my head before my own circumstances chased it away. He could have been anywhere, doing anything. A glimmer of hope lingered that he was still searching for me, but the world was vast, and I was small. Finding me would be like searching for a needle in a haystack. As we approached a set of ornately carved double doors, I really despised feeling like a needle. Yet, one thought crossed my mind as a deep male voice called from the other side, granting us permission to enter: Needles may be small, but they're still sharp enough to hurt. I clung to this thought, a small beacon of hope in the darkness of my situation.

I clenched my teeth together until my jaw ached as the door swung open. The male who awaited us on the other side was nothing like I had expected. The master of the manor appeared young, at least in looks. In fae terms, however, that meant little. He might have seemed only thirty, but that could easily translate to hundreds for a fae male.

Lord Argall's hair was blond, nearly white, and would have reached the middle of his back if not for the ponytail that hung against his nape. His hair color stood in sharp contrast to the solid black of his tunic and trousers, which fit perfectly against his tall, broad frame. He was no stranger to sparring and physical training, as evidenced by the sword strapped to his side. The bright turquoise of his eyes reminded me of the sea under the midday sun. It sickened me to realize that the slave owner, the man responsible for the subjugation and abuse of human women, was also handsome.

I was alone with the nobleman as the door closed behind me. Blinking, I forced myself to stop staring at his disarming smile, the same smile that possibly belonged to the male who had harmed Raven just hours earlier. While I couldn't be sure if his fists had struck the woman's battered face—especially as his own bronzed knuckles appeared clean and unmarred—I had no way of knowing for sure. His presence was suffocating, and I could feel my fear of him becoming more palpable by the second.

"Welcome," he said, his voice as smooth as butter. Blinking again, I lifted my gaze to the lord's handsome face. Looking him in the eyes was challenging, especially since my fear of him had become so palpable. "Elianna, is it?"

I nodded, unsure whether to speak up or remain silent. Lord Argall seemed to sense my hesitation, perhaps even reading it in my mind. The way his head tilted to one side indicated he was studying me, which only made me feel more vulnerable. Wrapping my arms around my chest, the low neckline of my gown doing little to hide my minimal cleavage, I scanned the room, trying to avoid looking directly at him.

It was clear he spared no expense on the finer things in life. The room we were in appeared ostentatious and impractical. Having spent my entire life in the human world, with its modern technology and fast-paced lifestyle, I felt as if I had gone back in time instead of simply crossing into another world. Perhaps I had done both, and I realized there was nothing simple about it.

Lord Argall's private wing of the manor was akin to his own apartment. Multiple doors, both open and closed, led to other parts of the suite from where we stood. The room reminded me of one of the sitting rooms I'd come across while touring historic estates and castles with my family. Just thinking about my parents threatened to rip my heart from my chest, but I tried to focus on happy memories—like how they took me to every museum imaginable to educate me, even if those memories could never be relived.

Priceless artwork adorned every wall, each piece a masterpiece. None depicted the lord's family, however. Most of the paintings were nature scenes or abstract shapes like those I had only seen in art museums—a reminder of my parents that haunted me.

"Do you have much art where you come from?" The closeness of Lord Argall's voice surprised me. Lost in my thoughts, I hadn't even noticed him approach. He was like a snake in the grass, sneaking up on his prey and waiting to strike. My skin prickled with discomfort.

"Yes." I took a few steps back, reestablishing the distance his approach had just removed. Suddenly, the porcelain vase on the shelf became the most interesting thing in the room. I admired it; the colorful pattern stood out against the white background as I avoided his gaze. For a moment, I wondered if I could use it to knock him over the head if he tried to touch me. After what had happened to Raven that morning, hitting him with anything is a bad idea. "Mostly in museums... artwork like this, I mean. My home had a lot of pictures of my family."

The room was too quiet, my thoughts too loud. I wondered where his wife was, but didn't dare to ask, wishing instead for another person to break the awkward silence. There was little for us to talk about. Unless he offered to return my key and help me find my mate, I had no use for his words, and he had no use for mine. He let out a breath, the sound grating on my nerves, before he held out his hand for me to take. I looked away, hugging my arms tighter around my chest.

"I believe my servants have a meal ready in the dining room." The lord cleared his throat, his hand still extended, waiting for me to take it, but mine remained tucked safely against my body. "Shall we?"

My defensive body language was unmistakable, but Lord Argall didn't comment on it. Instead, he turned on his heel, leading the way toward one of the open doorways as I followed behind like a timid puppy, my proverbial tail firmly between my legs.

The aroma of home-cooked food greeted me before I even stepped into the dining room. It made my stomach grumble, betraying my desire to refuse anything he offered me. We had been fed in the human quarters, and I had eaten some stew in the kitchen with Jenny the day before, but the spread across the large, dark wood table looked fit for royalty. Over the years, I had grown increasingly thin, my meals often coming back up due to my medication and treatments. My body craved the mouth-watering scents wafting through the room—roasted meats and vegetables, pastas, soups, and salads, all beautifully presented on elegant platters.

The lord pulled out a chair, waiting for me to sit. Once I did, he pushed my chair in and took his own seat at the head of the table. His gentlemanly behavior was a stark contrast to the man I had expected him to be, the one I knew he truly was. His eyes bore into the side of my face as I watched steam rise from the nearest dish, twirling and spinning until it disappeared into the air. I knew it was dangerous to ignore the lord as I was, risking his anger. Still, I found it impossible to acknowledge his presence any other way. Zoe's words flitted through my mind, reminding me of my priorities: Whatever you do, survive tonight.

I had to pull myself together if I wanted to live to see another day and have hope of being there when my mate found me. Battling my inner turmoil, I dropped my arms from around my chest. I lifted my eyes to the male beside me, managing a hesitant smile. It didn't reach my eyes, but it would have to suffice.

"Sorry," I said. "It's been hard to be away from my family."

Leaving my family wasn't the actual reason for my rudeness, but it felt like the most believable, inoffensive excuse I could offer. If he could read my mind, he would know I was lying. I hoped that wasn't one of the lord's fae powers as I waited for him to respond. I decided to ask the others about his abilities later; if he had powers, I needed to know what they were and how they worked before I could formulate a plan to retrieve my key.

He smiled back at me, but the gesture did little to ease my fear. "That's understandable. I can imagine it's difficult to leave your world."

Before I was forced to respond, a servant entered through one of the doors, approaching the table quietly and filling two golden plates with portions of food. Her white shift dress was spotless, and her blond hair was tied back into a tight bun at the top of her head. I studied the girl, who looked to be no older than a teenager, as she set Lord Argall's plate in front of him and then placed the other down in front of me.

"Thank you, Tabitha," he said, his voice stern but not unkind. Observing their interaction, I realized the girl was at least part-human, her ears rounded like mine, but her eyes were silver—definitely not human. With her face turned downward in submission, she nodded as the lord spoke. "That will be all."

Just as quickly as she entered, the young servant left, never once looking me in the eye. I pondered over her when the door closed, leaving me alone with the lord again. I wondered how someone so young had found herself as a servant in the lord's manor, if that's indeed what her position was.

Humans were not given the enchanted key until they reached legal adulthood—at least, that was what I had always thought. I didn't know the servant's age, but she didn't seem old enough to have received a key. However, with her silver eyes, she might not be human at all. I made another mental note to ask the others about the young half-human servants.

A glass of wine was placed in front of me, pulling me from my thoughts.

The dinner passed in a blur, with my conversation with Lord Argall mostly one-sided and lacking depth. He asked me about my health, though I suspected it was more to determine if I was fit enough to sell rather than out of any genuine concern for my well-being. I considered lying and telling him I was still sick, but he would have seen through my deception. If I wanted to survive the night, I needed to keep him entertained until he grew bored with me and sent me away. That was my hope, anyway, until the conversation shifted from mundane topics to my future in his custody.

"My healers told me you're pure." The lord's words made my stomach sink and twist in on itself.

When I looked up to meet his gaze, he was scrutinizing me. All I wanted to do was run away and hide, but I couldn't. "Pure?"

His amusement at my single-word response was evident. The corner of his mouth turned up in a smirk, and he nodded. "Pure," he echoed, as if I hadn't heard him the first time.

I had heard his revolting question, but I didn't think my sexual history was any business of his. Realization swept over me like a tidal wave of dread as I struggled to steady my shallow breaths. "As in untouched? Have you ever been to a male's bed, Elianna? I find it hard to believe that no man has taken you. For a human, your appearance is... pleasing."

I didn't know whether to thank him for the compliment or be sick. My throat tightened, a reminder of when my lungs had been too diseased to function. Still, I willed myself to maintain an impassive expression, unfazed by his questioning. "Does it matter whether I've been touched?"

His half-grin spread into a full smile at my blunt inquiry, pure amusement lighting up his face as he drained the rest of his wine. I had lost count of how many glasses he had consumed, but it was a significant number. "Yes, Elianna. It means you're worth more—more than most of the women here."

The drumming of my panicked heart only made it harder to breathe, my head threatening to spin. "Worth more to whom?"

I understood the implication but decided to play dumb. Perhaps if I acted immature and gave the impression of being too young, he would treat me accordingly and not expect me to do things I wasn't comfortable with. Of course, it was a foolish hope.

Sensing my unease, his amusement shifted to contemplation as he set his glass down on the table. My wine sat untouched in front of me. The last thing I needed was to lose my inhibitions around him, and I had no idea how the fae wine would affect me.

"Don't worry, Elianna. You'll be taken care of."

I doubted that, especially when he twisted in his chair, moving so close that our knees nearly touched. I tried to push myself back, but my chair was too heavy for me.

"It's actually why I wanted to meet with you tonight."

Though we were knee to knee, the lord's voice seemed distant as pressure built in my head, muffling the impact of his words. He watched me intently, his heavy-lidded gaze making my stomach churn.

"One of my concubines has become... troublesome. You will replace her."

What happened next was too quick for me to comprehend. The pressure in my head and the pounding in my chest heightened my awareness. My limbs tensed as my eyes locked onto his hand as it inched toward my leg.

In an instant, Lord Argall's palm touched my thigh, the slit in my dress revealing my skin. In the next moment, he was across the room, pressed against the wall by forces unknown.

"No," I said instinctively, a reaction I hadn't anticipated since I wanted to survive more than anything else. My entire body trembled as burning anger distorted Lord Argall's previously handsome face, though there was also a hint of fear.

The sound of boots stomping behind me marched in time with the pounding beat inside my head and heart. Before I could process what was happening, everything went black.

CHAPTER FOURTEEN

Blaze

The sun was already rising to its highest point in the sky when I woke up, feeling more exhausted than I had when I closed my eyes. The time for actual rest would come when I held my mate in my arms, inhaling the scent of her skin as she nestled into my chest. Just the thought of waking up with her body against mine made me harden, and various parts of me stirred at the most inopportune moment. With the Oathorne father and his two sons just outside my tent, it wasn't the right time for seeking release, not until I could provide it for her. So, pushing aside the uncomfortable needs of my body, I got out of the bedroll and stepped out of my tent, wrapping my cloak around myself to conceal the tightness of my trousers. I had a lot to accomplish before the auction the following day, so I couldn't afford to waste any more time.

Saying goodbye to the Oathorne family was tough. Although I hadn't known them long, I embraced them as any brother would before I left. It wasn't a proper goodbye. We had agreed on that ahead of time. The rest of my group decided to stay back for a few hours to give me a head start. I knew where to find them once I located my mate and our lives settled down.

We made tentative plans to meet a few days later, neither I nor the Oathorne males wanting to risk traveling through the forest alone. Since Baltair and his sons would need to pass through my home court to reach their own, it was another reason to ride together. Not only would we be safer in larger numbers—something essential to me since I hoped to be traveling with my mate—but it would also provide the Oathhornes with a place to rest during their long journey. My cottage and property were spacious enough to host them for a few nights to regain their strength for the rest of their trip, and I felt indebted to them for all the hospitality they had shown me.

It was a solid plan, but only if everything unfolded as I intended. If I couldn't find my mate, or if it took longer to free her than I expected, I knew the father and sons would have to leave the city without us. Acknowledging that it might not be possible for us to meet afterward, we still set up a tentative plan, agreeing on a day and location to meet before leaving the city together. I had three days to find my mate, rescue her, and meet my friends at the site of our last camp in the forest, or they would have to leave Cloudfell without me.

As I crept through the trees and underbrush, I returned to the main road, which was much busier than it had been the night before. With the sun high in the sky, the dirt path cutting through the trees was bustling with activity. People on foot, horseback, and even in carriages all traveled along the road, most heading toward the city of Cloudfell. I wasn't surprised by the traffic; Cloudfell was the largest city in the Court of Knowledge, attracting visitors for numerous reasons, particularly its markets, which offered a variety of products from around the realm.

As I approached the forest's edge, my steps slowed, and the centerpiece of the city came into view. Four imposing cylindrical towers of the elegant palace reached nearly to the clouds. Massive white stone walls, the same color as the palace, encased the structure in a protective block, with gold flags fluttering in the breeze above. Statues of past monarchs lined the perimeter of the property, with guards positioned among them. I passed the palace quickly, not wanting to linger in any one spot for too long. After the attack in the forest, I didn't want to risk being recognized if someone had sent my description to the city before I arrived.

One thing that surprised me about the traffic moving into the city was the number of convoys escorting nobles from across the four courts. The uniformed guards made it clear that these elite visitors were transporting valuable items either to or from the Court of Knowledge. I recognized the midnight blue flag of my own court, the Court of Harmony. I had marched under that same flag when I was a soldier in the war against the Court of Chaos.

I was no fool. It only took me a moment to realize that the wealthy from each court, those traveling with guards for protection, were there to buy human females to take back to their homelands. The flesh trade ran deeper than I had realized, with support from influential figures in each court. Pulling my hood tighter around my face, I directed Shadow to veer away from the guards, carriages, and wagons that had gathered near the city's gates.

The sight of nobles accompanied by so many guards to protect the human females they intended to purchase sparked an idea in my mind. Those planning to bid on and buy women would want their guards to keep an eye on their investments, perhaps even before the women were brought out into the auction. I grinned beneath my hood as a way onto the lord's property formed in my mind. All I needed was a uniform.

I secured Shadow to a cluster of trees near the outer wall of the city and sneaked behind the wagons of one of the convoys, which bore the crimson flags of the Court of Chaos. Of all the courts I expected to see in Cloudfell, Chaos had been the last. The War of the Four Courts had ended many years prior, and any alliance would have been fragile. Nevertheless, it was evident that even the Court of Knowledge's former enemy had been welcomed into the city to buy human women. I shuddered at the thought of my mate ending up in the hands of my former enemy.

As a pair of guards passed by, I ducked behind the wagon and slipped my head beneath the canvas covering the goods inside. The first wagon held mostly metalware, including swords and daggers. I was searching for uniforms but couldn't resist slipping two daggers into my bandolier. Once the guards moved on, engrossed in conversation about visiting the brothel, I slipped out from under the wagon's cover and moved to the next one in line.

I had to search through three more wagons before I found one containing extra guard uniforms. The Court of Chaos may have been in Cloudfell for the auction, but they had brought plenty of goods to trade. I took two complete uniforms, including boots, cloaks, and necessary accessories, stuffing them into a large bag before sneaking my haul back into the trees, where Shadow waited, happily grazing on the patch of grass beside her. After climbing back onto the saddle and rubbing her neck in gratitude for being a good girl, I set my sights on finding an inn.

There were multiple inns in the city, a natural benefit of Cloudfell being such a bustling place. The Drunk Swallow Inn was not what one would expect when visiting such a beautiful market city. Located five blocks away from the palace and far off the beaten path, I wasn't even sure if it was a legitimate business. From the outside, it appeared condemned or should have been. The building was half falling apart, and even the sign hung on only one hook, making me tilt my head to read it. Nevertheless, the downstairs tavern had an open sign, and I was starving, so I decided to take my chances and entered.

While the outside of the tavern may have appeared abandoned, the inside was more crowded than I would have liked or expected. Even with several blocks separating The Drunk Swallow Inn from the palace at the city's center, people had come to this rough-around-the-edges tavern just like I had.

I left my hood on as I approached the bar, taking the stool closest to the wall, and ordered a bowl of stew and an ale. With my spy's ears tuned in to the conversations around me, I listened for more information about the upcoming auction.

The chatter in the tavern was overwhelming, making it difficult to focus on a single conversation or determine which ones were the most crucial. I realized that most of the patrons were locals, people who frequented the tucked-away bar, even when the city wasn't filled with outsiders. The barkeep stayed busy, wiping down surfaces and refilling glasses, rarely stopping to chat with his customers. Perhaps he was too busy, or maybe he felt uncomfortable with the crowd drawn to his city for such a grim purpose. I wondered how the city's residents thought about the flesh trade happening so close to their homes—especially families with children.

One bite of the stew in front of me made me realize why the locals frequented such a rundown tavern. Just like the tavern in the forest, the cook had taken great care to prepare the midday meal. The meat and vegetables in the stew were cut into generous chunks; it was a stew, not merely a watery excuse for a meal. I devoured the stew but sipped my ale slowly, wanting to keep a clear head as I plotted.

The word "auction" never came up in any of the conversations I overheard, but something else captured my attention.

A group of four men sat at a small table in the corner of the room, talking amongst themselves. They were dressed in fine clothing, which didn't quite match the attire of the bar's regulars, who wore clothes meant for fieldwork and labor. I twisted on my stool, finding a better angle to hear their conversation clearly.

"They'll be circulating through the crowd tonight," one man said, his voice low but filled with excitement.

"All of them?" another asked, to which a sound of affirmation followed from one of his companions.

"But the masks? Lord Argall is probably trying to sell off the most unfortunate-looking ones by hiding their faces so we won't know better."

The men were discussing a party, one where women who were to be auctioned off would mingle in the crowd for the men to look at and interact with. Fiery rage built in my chest, but I forced myself to continue listening.

"I don't think you have enough options to be picky. If you want an heir, you'll need a female. Just put a bag over her face if she's not to your liking, as long as the other parts of her work."

My hands tightened into fists. I wanted to stand up from the bar, walk across the room, and punch the man who had said something so disgusting. He deserved to wear a bag over his head instead. But I remained where I was, willing the fire in my blood to cool.

By the time I pulled myself together and looked up from my hands, which were white-knuckled against the bar, the four men had already walked out the door. I no longer had a day to prepare for the auction since I had just learned there would be a party that night, one where my mate would probably be forced to mingle with potential slave traders. I slid a few coins across the table and rented a room at the inn for the night. Taking the key from the barkeep, who barely acknowledged me, I slung my pack over my shoulder and climbed the stairs to the second floor.

The room was small, the bed barely large enough for even one full-sized fae male, but I didn't plan to stay there long. Dropping the bag containing the uniforms onto the bed, I entered the tiny bathing room and filled the basin with water. The tub in the corner looked inviting, but I couldn't spare the additional time to fill it. I stripped off my dirty tunic and trousers, debating whether they needed to be burned. Using a soapy rag and water, I cleaned my skin as best as I could, brushed my teeth, and finger-combed my hair, tying it back with a strip of leather.

Once I was clean enough for the limited time I had,

I put on the stolen uniform, cringing at having to wear the Court of Chaos' colors. Part of me felt like a traitor for losing many of my own people to Chaos' swords. Still, I had my reasons for taking uniforms from their wagons rather than from one of the other courts. The Court of Chaos had sent nearly double the number of guards compared to the others, which allowed me to blend better into the crowd. With relations still strained and mistrust rampant between the courts, the nobles from the Court of Knowledge undoubtedly wouldn't want to anger former enemies by denying their guards the opportunity to do their jobs as their lords saw fit.

So, wearing the same colors as the men I had slain in battle, I exited the tavern through the back door, stepping into the dark alley as a Court of Chaos guard, heading to Lord Argall's party like all the others dressed just like me.

CHAPTER FIFTEEN

Elianna

The sound of talking woke me, but I couldn't make out any of the words as I opened my eyes. I was back in my bed, but I wasn't sure how I had gotten there. The last thing I remembered was sitting in a chair at Lord Argall's dining table. He had reached to place his hand on my leg, and then... Gasping, my hand shot up to cover my mouth as the memory flooded back. When the lord had tried to touch me, an invisible force had thrown him across the room and held him against the wall. I couldn't suppress a shudder as I recalled the furious look on his face. He would kill me, I realized.

Throwing the blankets off, I checked my arms and legs and ran my hands along my face, but there were no injuries. I hadn't been harmed.

So caught up in searching myself for wounds and trying to understand what I had experienced the night before, I hadn't noticed the tiny creature with chaotic brown hair and a floppy brown hat until he tried to pull the pillow from behind me.

"Pith! You scared me!" I exclaimed, scanning the chambers, but again, it was just me and the brownie in the room.

He scoffed. "Pith cannot help it if he is ugly enough to scare you, Miss Lazy Bones, but I still need you to move your lazy bones so I can make this bed."

Fighting back a grin, I climbed off the bed and slid my feet into my slippers before moving a few steps away. "I wasn't scared of you because of your appearance, Pith. You startled me because I didn't know anyone was there until you got so close."

The brownie seemed to ignore me as he fluffed my pillows and smoothed the blankets over the bed, mumbling to himself once more. "No one cares about Pith's chores until he doesn't do them on time. Pith has so much work to do for Master's party today, and everyone sleeps like lazy bones. Then Pith can't make their beds on time when he still needs to clean Master's quarters to make a good impression on his friends. But is anyone Pith's friend? No. Pith has no friends because they call him ugly and say he scares them."

How the creature spoke to himself, engaging in long monologues as if he were speaking both sides of the conversation, had me covering my mouth to stifle a giggle. The last thing I wanted was for him to think I was making fun of him. "Hey, Pith? Can I ask you something?"

The brownie turned, his wrinkled face scrunching up as he lifted a bushy black eyebrow over eyes that were much too large for his face. "You mean to talk to Pith, Miss Lazy Bones?"

I grinned and curtsied in front of him. He seemed to appreciate the gesture and dipped his head, the pointy end of his hat flopping over in front of his face. "I heard you saying that you clean the Master's rooms, Pith. Can I ask you something about that?"

The brownie turned back to my bed, fluffing the pillows as if he was deliberately avoiding my question. The nervousness in his movements was evident. I moved forward, stepping around him to sit back on the bed. He huffed loudly, making his irritation evident.

"Pith, can I ask you a tiny question about the Master's quarters? It can be our little secret." He shot a hesitant glance at me before quickly averting his eyes.

"Do you know what I think is so great, Pith?"

His face returned to mine, the expectant look making his eyes seem as large as dinner plates. "Yes, Miss Lazy Bones. Do you think Pith is great?"

I grinned. "I think it's really great that Pith can disappear and reappear wherever he likes. I wish I had that magic. You must be very powerful." I had never seen Pith's smile before, and I hoped to never see it again, but the mouth full of incredibly sharp, yellow teeth told me he was enjoying my compliments. I needed him to continue the conversation, so I smiled back at him.

"Pith is a very powerful brownie. Pith can even appear in places where magic is not supposed to go." Clearly, his magic was a point of pride, as his chest puffed out with those last words.

Nodding, I set my face to portray awe. "I didn't even think that was possible, Pith. That's really impressive." His chest remained puffed out, his eyes bright with pride. I had his attention, but I wasn't sure how long I would keep it if I asked him about Lord Argall's chambers again. Still, I had to try. "So, does that mean you're able to visit the room with the magical keys?"

I watched the brownie's expression, hoping it wouldn't change when he realized I was manipulating him, but it remained steady. "Pith is definitely powerful enough to see the shiny keys. Master doesn't like people to go there, but Pith still goes sometimes because Pith likes how they light up in the dark like they're alive."

"Oh, Pith!" I exaggerated my excitement, and it worked. His eyes lit up like a glowing green moon. "How I would love to see that! It sounds beautiful."

"Oh, it is, Miss Lazy Bones. Pith will take you one day, when it is safe." He turned his head toward the door just moments before the doorknob jiggled. "Pith must clean, Miss Lazy Bones. Pith will return to talk to you soon."

With a snap of his fingers, the brownie disappeared, but my hope was renewed, if only slightly. I threw myself back on my bed, feeling warmth and comfort fill me. However, when the door opened, I expected to see Zoe, not Hiedra.

"Ah, Miss Elianna, you're awake." The servant narrowed her eyes at me as she shut the door behind her. "You and I need to have a talk."

Memories of what happened the night before rushed back to me, threatening to push my newfound hope away. "About what? Did something happen? To Raven? To Zoe?"

The look in Hiedra's eyes was softer than I had ever seen. She scanned the room before approaching the bed, sitting on the edge, and speaking low enough to avoid being overheard. "Do you remember what happened last night, Miss?"

I shook my head, trying to piece together the fragments of memory that didn't make sense. Nothing seemed clear after the lord attempted to touch me.

"Master Argall was thrown against the wall of his dining room, Miss Elianna. Do you remember that happening?"

I nodded, tears streaming down my cheeks as fear washed over me. What could Hiedra's visit mean? "I remember, but I don't know how it happened. I didn't touch him. I swear he doesn't think I did that to him, does he?"

The corner of Hiedra's lilac mouth curled into a smile. She wiped a tear from my cheek with her thumb—the first act of kindness she had ever shown me. "But you did do that to him, Miss Elianna. Although I don't think you understand how you did it."

I slid my arms behind me and propped myself up on my elbows. "What do you think I did to him? When he flew against the wall and was held there, he was suspended in mid-air, with nothing holding him. It was like... magic." I shook my head vigorously. "I don't have magic, Hiedra."

The knowing smile on Hiedra's face suggested she knew far more than what she was revealing. "You have magic. I ensured that when I healed you."

Her words didn't quite register at first. I blinked, waiting for her to elaborate.

"When they brought you here, you were very sick. No one was sure if you were well enough for our healing."

I sat up straighter, scratching my head and blinking again, as if seeing more clearly would help me understand better. "Are you saying you healed me? I thought you were just a servant."

Stretching her back, Hiedra nodded. "I'm many things in this manor, Miss. I healed you and gave you a little more of my power. I did this partly because you needed it to survive, and partly because I hoped that if you were strong enough to survive such a terrible illness, you'd also be strong enough to free them."

I leaned forward, every statement from Hiedra urging me to get closer. It struck me how dangerous Hiedra's admissions were—how severely she would be punished if the lord discovered what she had done or was saying. "The other human women? You gave me the power, hoping I could free them? All of them?"

Hiedra leaned closer until our faces were mere inches apart, her obsidian eyes reflecting her determination. "I did, but you won't be able to do it all at once. Before you can gain the allies needed to save the others—both present and future—you must first save yourself."

My heart raced in my chest, and I rubbed my hands down my face, feeling dizzy from the pressure in my head. "How do I save myself? You saw what happened to Raven. I can't escape. There's no way out."

Hiedra smiled, though the expression didn't soothe my rising anxiety. "There's a party tonight, Miss Elianna. You will go."

"What does the party have to do with anything, Hiedra? I don't understand any of this. And what about what happened with Lord Argall? Isn't he going to have me killed for attacking him? I don't even know how I did it."

Setting a lilac hand on my knee, Hiedra lowered her voice even more. "Lord Argall no longer wants you as a concubine. Your ability to repel someone, to control where they are, terrifies him. Even though he isn't entirely sure it was you who did it, he still wants you out of his manor as soon as possible. He wants you to become someone else's problem. He won't kill you, although I know that's your fear. Your purity and age make you incredibly valuable. You'll attend the party tonight to be presented to other nobles who may want to purchase you."

Dread built in my chest at Hiedra's words, bile crawling up my throat. "How will I manage to escape if I'm purchased by someone else?"

"It won't go that far, Miss Elianna, but you need to listen carefully, and this must stay between us." I nodded, my eyes unblinking as I focused on her serious expression. "When I leave this room, you'll eat something, then go to the bathing room to let the servants prepare you for the ball. When it's time for the party, you'll go. You'll look lovely, act charming, and mind your manners. You'll mingle with the crowd, but avoid getting too close to any of the males here who are buying women. Be present, but not available. You need to delay leaving the party. Even if you must hide in a bathing room or a closet, you should stay at the party as long as you can."

I nodded, though I felt more confused than before. "How does staying at the party help me escape?"

Tipping her head to the side, Hiedra snapped her fingers. With a pop, Pith appeared, holding a golden key in his hand. My heart skipped a beat at the sight. He grinned and winked at me before handing the key to Hiedra, then disappeared again.

"You need to stay at the party as long as you can, Miss Elianna, because the moment I put this key back into your hand, your mate will know you're here, and I don't think he'll let anything stand in the way of finding you. I can tell just by the power humming through it that he's close—really close. He'll come for you, but I don't want him to be too late. Other nobles will be at the party, and if they discover you—your purity—they'll be throwing coins at Lord Argall, eager to buy you before the auction. So, do your best to remain unnoticed by them and keep a close eye on this key. You'll know when he's getting closer. You'll feel the connection... and when the time is right, come back stronger, with allies, and be a savior for all the women who've lost their freedoms."

I didn't know how to respond, but I reached for Hiedra, taking her hand. "Why are you helping us?"

Her lips lifted into a small smile as she squeezed my fingers. "I've never stopped helping you, Miss. You just didn't know it."

CHAPTER SIXTEEN

Elianna

The golden key sprang to life when it touched my hand, the familiar hum of magic nearly bringing me to tears. After everything I had experienced over the past week, I could never have imagined that Hiedra was on our side, but she was. The thought of the winged female transferring power to me lingered at the back of my mind, but the metal object in my hand drew my full attention. Hiedra had left me alone in the bedchamber moments after placing the key in my hand, and I had yet to move. I couldn't. All I could do was stand in the middle of the room and watch the key flash like a beacon. He would come for me.

The twisting of the doorknob jolted me back to reality, a momentary warning to hide the key before I was caught with it and it was taken away from me again. I dropped to the floor, sliding the key into my slipper just before Zoe entered the room.

"Oh, good. You're awake," Zoe said as she closed the door behind her. The rapid beating of my heart calmed at the sight of my friend. I wished I could tell her about the key, about Hiedra's plans, but it was too dangerous. I couldn't tell anyone—not if I wanted to escape without getting caught. "Hiedra said you were sick, so I've been bunking in another room."

I nodded. I was a terrible liar, so omission was the safest way to respond.

Pulling my dress over my head, I paused as the key continued to pulse beneath my foot. "Will you be getting ready for the party?" I asked.

Zoe nodded, reaching out her hand. "I was waiting so we could go together. Are you ready? Do you need more time?"

Her thoughtfulness made me feel even guiltier. If I told anyone, I had to tell Zoe. I didn't know if I could live with myself if I didn't, so I pulled my best friend into a hug and decided to share everything with her.

After I shared with Zoe the power that Hiedra had given me while healing, the key, and the escape plan, my friend's blue eyes looked as wide as a deer caught in headlights. A few moments of silence passed before Zoe responded. "I'm going to help you get out."

My heart lifted at her words, but I shook my head and spoke softly. "No, Zoe. We'll get out together."

"Elianna," Zoe said, her hands rising to cradle my face. "Hiedra is right. There's too much risk if more than one of us tries to leave."

All I could do was shake my head as I stared at my hands, the overwhelming emotions of the situation burning in the backs of my eyes.

Letting go of my face, Zoe pulled me into a hug, whispering into my ear, "Listen to me when I say that I'll be okay. I'm not going anywhere. Find your male and bring back a whole damn army to get us out." Tears fell as Zoe's words soaked into the fabric of her dress. "Until then, someone has to stay here and look out for the rest of the girls."

We left shortly after that, and I didn't want to say goodbye to my friend as I wiped away my tears and finished dressing. I had lost my appetite and bypassed the table with the bread and cheese laid out, heading instead to meet the guards at the door so we could be escorted to the bathing chamber.

With the masked party only hours away, nearly

every woman owned by Lord Argall was in the bathing room at some stage of getting ready, even those like Zoe, who usually worked in the brothel. From what Zoe had told me, he wanted all the girls present to offer the visiting dignitaries more options to choose from—not just women to take back home with them. Instead of the nobles visiting the brothel, the lord intended to bring the brothel to them. The thought made bile burn in the back of my throat, even though I knew my purity made me off-limits for that kind of use. I didn't like the idea of my friend being used in such a way, either.

Steam billowed from five large tubs, with Jenny and at least ten other women already in them. Several others sat at various vanities, fixing their hair and makeup. What surprised me was the numerous young servants in the room, including the one who had served me and Lord Argall our food the night before. They all looked young, perhaps too young.

I nudged Zoe toward the pool with the fewest occupants and pulled off my dress, stepping into the warm water. My key was safely tucked inside my slipper next to the pool, with my clean undergarments sitting on top to hide it from view.

There were two other women in the tub we had chosen, neither of whom I had spent much time with before. One woman, Aliyah, was stunning, her rich brown skin making her golden eyes shine even brighter. With her curvy figure and sultry voice, it was no surprise she worked in the brothel alongside Zoe—she would have certainly been desirable to most men.

The other woman had hair as black as Aliyah's, but it was razor-straight and cut to her chin, rather than hanging down her back in tight curls. She was introduced as Tegan, and she, too, had been assigned to the brothel. It seemed that most of Lord Argall's slaves were used in this capacity, unless selling them brought in more profit or they became more trouble than they were worth. I guessed I fit into both categories, especially after I had thrown him against the wall with a power I didn't know I had.

"Zoe?" I asked as I soaped my hair. "Who are all those servants? They look too young to have come from the human lands."

My friend grimaced, barely glancing over her shoulder at the young girl who had just dropped towels on the floor beside the pool. "That's because they didn't come from the human lands. The younger servants, those under seventeen, are all half-fae." I turned to look toward the side of the room, where one of the younger servants was braiding Lauren's dark brown hair. I hadn't seen Lauren since the morning I worked in the kitchens. When I turned back to Zoe, the other two women in our tub wore the same expression. "All the children born to those who get pregnant in the brothel are taken for servitude when they are old enough to wash dishes."

I swallowed, my stomach churning. "Are there many children born to women in the brothel?"

"More than will help you sleep well at night," Tegan responded, her tone reflecting her disgust. "They can make a tonic to prevent it, but that would defeat the purpose of bringing human women through the portal to help them repopulate."

With the unpleasant taste returning to my throat, I was glad I had skipped a meal. "That's awful."

"Yeah," Zoe said, glancing toward the door as it opened. Hiedra entered with Raven, the woman's face no longer bruised, but her shoulders were slumped as she shuffled in. The healers must have taken care of her physical wounds, but the emotional ones clearly remained. "If you take care of the pregnancy yourself, the healers usually keep it a secret."

The conversation made it increasingly hard for me to ignore the burning in my throat. "Take care of it ourselves?"

"Yeah... you know, the way women in our world did before there was a safer way." Rising from the tub, Zoe's body dripped water all over the tiles as she approached Raven and escorted her back to us.

As Zoe helped the black-haired girl into the tub, the conversation about pregnancies and abortion came to an end. Raven had been through enough over the past few days, so none of us wanted to upset her any further.

Aliyah and Tegan got out of the pool shortly after Raven entered, moving to the vanities where the servants waited to prepare them for the party. Racks of dresses had been brought in and stood against the back wall, with masquerade-style masks hanging from each one. I wasn't sure what to expect from a party filled with nobility from across the realm, but it was clear that no expense had been spared. The lord had plenty of money, and he seemed to enjoy showing it off.

Once Raven joined us in the tub, she said very little, her dark eyes revealing negligible life. Zoe didn't push her to talk. When she said she would remain behind to take care of the other women, she meant it. Even at her young age, the blonde seemed to be the mother of the group, always swooping in to help when their hands were shaking.

The thought of leaving my friend, even with all of Zoe's assurances, filled me with trepidation. Staying in the manor was scary, but leaving filled me with nearly as much fear. Hiedra had assured me that my mate was nearby and that he would come for me, but it didn't change the fact that I didn't know him. For all I knew, he might be one of the nobles visiting the manor to purchase a female. Just because he had the twin to my key didn't mean he was a good male, or that I would fall in love with him, or even find him attractive. The choices were being made for me, so I knew it didn't matter, but I couldn't help but wonder if I would have been better off staying where I was.

After a short time, the last of the bathing women, myself included, climbed out of the tubs. I dried quickly and slipped my feet into my slippers before even putting on my undergarments. The key vibrated against my foot, its sensation quickening my heart as I realized my mate was near. When I sat at an empty vanity, Zoe sitting in front of the mirror beside me, most of the other women had already been escorted out. The call of the enchanted metal inside my slipper was hard to ignore as a servant girl helped me with my hair and makeup, bringing over dress after dress for me to choose from.

Every gown was stunning, even more beautiful than the satin and lace one I had worn to dinner with Lord Argall. Knowing it would be the first outfit my mate ever saw me in made it impossible for me to choose.

After turning down six selections, with the dark-haired teen nearly out of breath from trying to sell me on each one, I finally settled on a full-length powder blue gown made of tulle and silk. It was covered in embroidered golden flowers that sparkled in the light. The bodice was fitted, while the skirt flared out at the waist. It was the most gorgeous gown I'd ever seen. Once the mask was placed on my face, with the sparkling gold accentuating the gold in my hair, I felt like a princess.

After slipping my feet into a pair of gold slippers, I covertly moved the key below the vanity with my toes, waiting while another servant readied Zoe and Raven. Zoe's cherry red ball gown was phenomenal, with much fluffier skirts than mine and a bodice covered in embroidered silver swirls. A silver mask was placed on Zoe's face, enhancing the brightness of her light blue eyes.

After Raven dressed in a violet gown selected by the servant, the three of us left the bathing chamber together, escorted by two male guards I hadn't seen before. The power of the key inside my shoe surged through me, tightening my stomach with its intensity.

We moved through the halls in silence, me mentally mapping out the familiar path as we were led into the central corridor that I knew led to the ballroom I had cleaned with Jenny just a few days prior. As we got closer, the halls became more congested, and the sounds of music filled the space. Dozens of guards in uniforms I hadn't seen before lined the halls on either side of the large wooden doors. My lungs struggled to pull in enough air as I focused on the humming of the object against my foot, the power within it willing me to calm. He was close. Aliyah and Tegan got out of the pool shortly after Raven entered, moving to the vanities and the servants who waited to ready them for the party. Racks of dresses had been brought in and stood against the back wall, masquerade-style masks hanging from each one. I didn't know what to expect from a party filled with nobility from across the realm, but it was clear no expense had been spared. The lord had plenty of money, and he seemed to enjoy showing it off.

With negligible life showing from behind her dark eyes, Raven said very little once she joined us in the tub. Zoe didn't push her. When Zoe said she would remain behind to take care of the other women, she meant it. Even with her young age, the blonde seemed to be the mother of the group, always swooping in to help them pick up the pieces when their hands were shaking.

The thought of leaving my friend, even after all Zoe's assurance, filled me with trepidation. Staying in the manor was scary, but leaving filled me with nearly as much fear. Hiedra had assured me that my mate was nearby and that he would come for me, but it didn't change the fact that I didn't know him. For all I knew, he was one of the nobles who would be visiting the manor to purchase a female. Just because he had the twin to my key didn't mean he was a good male, and it didn't mean I would fall in love with him, or even find him attractive. The choices were being made for me, so I knew it didn't matter, but I couldn't help but wonder if I would've been better off staying where I was.

The last of the bathing women, me included, climbed out of the tubs a short time after Raven was brought in. Drying quickly, I slipped my feet into my slippers before I'd even pulled on my undergarments. The key vibrated against my foot, the sensation revving up my heart, knowing that my mate was near. When I sat at a vacant vanity, Zoe sitting in front of the mirror beside me, most of the other women had already been escorted out. The call of the enchanted metal inside my slipper was hard to ignore as the servant girl helped me with my hair and makeup before bringing over dress after dress, giving me the option to choose.

Every gown was stunning, even more so than the satin and lace one I'd worn to dinner with Lord Argall. Knowing it would be the first outfit my mate ever saw me in, I couldn't choose..

After turning down six selections, the dark-haired teen, nearly out of breath from trying to sell me on each one, finally settled on a full-length powder blue gown made of tulle and silk. It was covered in embroidered golden flowers that sparkled in the light. The bodice was fitted, but the skirts flared out at the waist. It was the most gorgeous gown I'd ever seen. Once the mask was placed on my face, the sparkling gold bringing out the gold in my hair, I felt like a princess.

After slipping my feet into a pair of gold slippers, I moved the key covertly below the vanity with my toes, waiting as another servant readied Zoe and Raven. Zoe's own cherry red ball gown was phenomenal. The skirts were much fluffier than mine, and the entire bodice was covered in embroidered silver swirls. A silver mask was placed on Zoe's face, the color of which made her light blue eyes appear even brighter.

After Raven dressed, the servant chose a violet gown for her, and the three of us left the bathing chamber together, escorted by two male guards I hadn't seen before. The power of the key inside my shoe surged through me, my stomach tightening at the intensity of it.

We moved through the halls in silence, me mapping out the familiar path as we were led into the central corridor that I knew led to the ballroom I'd cleaned with Jenny only a few days prior. As we drew closer, the halls became increasingly congested, the sounds of music filling the space. Dozens of guards in uniforms I'd never seen before lined the halls on either side of the large wooden doors. My lungs not pulling in enough air, I focused on the humming of the object against my foot, the power inside it willing me to calm. *He* was close.

CHAPTER SEVENTEEN

Blaze

I stayed in the shadows as I returned to where I had left my horse, not wanting to draw attention to myself until I could blend into the ranks of the Court of Chaos. The guards were scattered across the city, taking their breaks in groups to enjoy the amenities. I easily found the largest group of Chaos guards, their crimson uniforms standing out in the late afternoon sun as they traveled in a loose formation down the main road toward the outskirts of the city. The helmet concealed most of my features, and the rest of the uniform appeared to be standard issue, so I was confident in my ability to blend in. Under my direction, Shadow kept pace with the outer line of guards. A few of the men nodded in my direction as we moved forward, not suspecting me to be anyone but one of their own.

As I made my way through the city's streets, I relied on my experience as a spy in the military to track the locations of the city guards, even those who were undercover. The Court of Knowledge may have invited nobles from other courts to their capital. Still, it was clear they didn't trust them, considering the number of guards peeking out of every shop window and down each street. Even without their uniforms, it was easy to recognize them in plain clothes, no matter how hard they tried to blend in—especially for someone who knew what to look for.

The businesses lining the main street were mostly those that opened during the day, with a few taverns scattered throughout. However, once we turned onto the road leading out of the city, the atmosphere changed. Like any large city, Cloudfell had its seedy parts, and they were extensive. There were several brothels, rundown inns, and taverns, the buildings in much worse shape than those near the palace.

I wondered if she was in one of those brothels, where off-duty guards walked in and out, but I didn't have time to explore that possibility. If Lord Argall was set to auction off human women the following night, that was my best lead, and I had to follow it, especially while my disguise was working. Passing by the businesses where I knew human women were being exploited churned my stomach. The thought of my mate being among them was unbearable. If she wasn't at the manor, I knew exactly where to look next, but I forced myself to keep my eyes forward, away from the crumbling buildings that contained such suffering.

The midnight businesses gave way to residential homes and estates as we traveled along the dirt road leading to the Emerald Sea. The sun had begun to set, and the temperature had dropped, leaving me chilly in the thin material of the Chaos uniform. It was warmer in their court, located at the southernmost tip of the continent. The cloak I wore provided some additional warmth, but the breeze still sent shivers along my skin. I took a deep breath, my heartbeat increasing in intensity as our pace slowed.

Power hummed through me as the convoy of three courts in front of me halted, creeping forward at a glacial pace as they undoubtedly reached their destination. My muscles twitched with the urge to break formation and rush forward to search for my mate, the desire battling against my sensibilities.

"If they don't start moving soon, I'm going to have to find a place to piss." The guard beside me, a younger male, caught me by surprise as he moved closer. Shadow, my horse, shifted beneath me, her instincts as alert as mine. If I were discovered, I would be completely outnumbered.

I forced a chuckle and nodded, my eyes shifting from the male beside me to the unmoving wagons and cavalry in front of us. Having an accent that marked me as being from the Court of Harmony, I didn't want to speak unless I had to.

"Are you looking forward to the party? We can't take a female home with us, but that doesn't mean we can't sample the goods. Commander Balhana said Lord Argall was bringing in women from the brothel, aside from those going up for auction." Anger burned in my gut, the desire to knock the other male off his horse palpable. Instead, I simply shook my head and smoothed my hand along Shadow's fur; she was visibly agitated.

The guard must have picked up on my disinterest in the conversation, because he shrugged and nudged his horse forward as the procession started moving again. The moment Shadow took her first step behind the others, I felt the power strumming through my limbs intensify, zeroing in on the pocket of my uniform. The key was calling to me. She was nearby. I could feel it.

My breath faltered as the enchanted object signaled the proximity of my mate, making it hard to breathe. I had worried for days that the key she held had been taken from her, but if it had been, it seemed she had gotten it back. My pocket pulsed with magic, my body vibrating with its force. I needed to touch it, to see it with my own eyes, but I couldn't—not as I marched alongside dozens of other guards heading toward the lord's estate for the night's party, which would introduce visiting nobility to the human women available for auction. Gripping the pommel of my sword, I tried to steady my breath. Even if she were there, I wouldn't be able to just walk into the manor and take her. It would be far too dangerous. The number of guards surrounding me made that clear.

Adrenaline surged through me as we moved forward another mile. The convoy in front of me disappeared when we made a right turn onto a long, forested driveway. I kept my hand on the key in my pocket, the feeling of urgency increasing as I moved closer.

The property was grand, surrounded by stone walls at least ten feet high, but the gates were open, allowing caravans from each court access to the grounds. They piled in, dozens of guards escorting the carriages and wagons onto the property and settling in the fields around the main gardens. I stayed behind, maneuvering Shadow into the tree line that framed three sides of the property's walls. I needed to see the enchanted key still humming in my pocket.

The forest surrounding the property was a small blessing. It allowed me to let Shadow loose while I was in the manor, knowing my whistle would call her back once I was ready to leave. I needed to stay off the radar, so I had to go on foot.

Walking her deep into the forest, far enough so guards wouldn't stumble upon us, I dismounted but didn't tie Shadow's reins to a tree. If she fell into danger or risked being taken by someone else, I wanted her to have the freedom to run.

Although the pounding of my heart matched the insistence of the key in my pocket, I scanned the surrounding forest to ensure I was alone before pulling the magical object from my pants. Once I did, my breath caught in my throat; my body urged me to run to her, while my mind told me to proceed cautiously. I'd seen guards stepping in and out of the front doors before I walked away to enter the forest, so I knew I could get into the manor. What I would do once inside was the question that lingered as I pressed the cool metal against my lips before sliding it back into my pocket.

The vibrations coming from inside my pocket grew more urgent as I made my way back onto the estate grounds on foot, Shadow safely grazing in the forest behind me. My heart tightened painfully at the realization that both my life and my mate's were hanging in the balance, creating a noticeable pressure in my chest.

"If they don't start moving soon, I'm going to have to find a place to relieve myself." The guard beside me, a younger male from what I could tell, caught me off guard as he moved closer. Shadow shifted beneath me, her instincts on alert just like mine. If I were discovered, I would be completely outnumbered.

I forced a chuckle and nodded, my eyes leaving the male beside me to glance toward the unmoving wagons and cavalry in front of us. With my accent marking me as someone from the Court of Harmony, I didn't want to speak unless absolutely necessary.

"Are you looking forward to the party? We can't take a female home with us, but that doesn't mean we can't sample the goods. Commander Balhana said Lord Argall was bringing in women from the brothel, aside from those going up for auction." Fire burned in my gut; my desire to knock the other male off his horse was palpable. Instead, I shook my head and smoothed my hand along Shadow's fur, who was visibly agitated.

The guard pestering me must have noticed my disinterest in the conversation, as he shrugged and nudged his horse forward when the procession began to move again. The moment Shadow took her first step behind the others, the power thrumming through my limbs increased, zeroing in on the pocket of my uniform. The key was calling to me. She was nearby. I could feel it.

My breath faltered, the enchanted object signaling the proximity of my mate, making it hard to breathe. I had worried for days that the key she held had been taken away from her, but if it had been, it seemed she had gotten it back. My pocket pulsed with magic, my own body vibrating with its force. I needed to touch it, to see it with my own eyes, but I couldn't. Not as I marched alongside dozens of other guards, all heading toward the lord's estate where the night's party would introduce visiting nobility to the human women available for purchase at the auction. I gripped the pommel of my sword, trying to steady my breath. Even if she were there, there would be no way I could just walk into the manor and take her. It would be dangerous. The number of guards surrounding me made that clear.

My adrenaline surged as we moved forward another mile, the convoy in front of me disappearing when we made a right turn onto a long, forested driveway. I gripped the key through the fabric, feeling its pulsing energy intensify as I drew closer.

The property was palatial, surrounded by stone walls at least ten feet high, but the gates were open, allowing carriages and wagons from each court access to the grounds. They piled in, dozens of guards escorting them onto the property, settling them in the fields around the main gardens. I stayed behind, maneuvering Shadow into the treeline that framed three sides of the property's walls. I needed to set eyes on the enchanted key still humming in my pocket; I had to see for myself that it was calling to me.

The forest surrounding the property was a small blessing. It allowed me to set Shadow loose while I was in the manor, knowing my whistle would call her back once I was ready to leave. I needed to stay off the radar, so I decided to go on foot.

Walking her deep into the forest, I ventured far enough away from the guards who might need to relieve themselves. I dismounted but did not tie Shadow's reins to a tree. If she were to face danger or risk being taken by someone else, I wanted her to have the freedom to run.

Although my heart raced in tandem with the key pressing against my pocket, I scanned the surrounding forest to ensure I was alone before retrieving the magical object from my pants. As I pulled it out, my breath caught in my throat; my instincts urged me to run to her, but my mind reminded me to proceed cautiously. I had noticed the guards coming in and out of the front doors before I entered the forest, so I knew I could access the manor. The question of what to do once inside loomed in my mind as I pressed the cool metal against my lips before safely tucking it back into my pocket.

The vibrations from the key inside my pocket grew more urgent as I walked back onto the estate grounds on foot, leaving Shadow safely grazing in the forest behind me. A painful squeeze gripped my heart as the realization hit me that both my life and my mate's depended on my following actions, creating a heavy pressure in my chest.

Ahead, the large double doors of the manor loomed, flanked by guards, while others moved in and out of the property. The sun had already set, casting the edges of the estate into the moonlit darkness, but torchlight illuminated the grounds along with various bonfires that the guards had built near their convoys. Tents were already erected in scattered groups, a clear indication that the nobles of the court expected to be at the party until the early morning hours. Anxiety gnawed at me as I worried about my mate being taken by one of the visiting nobles, both for the night and for the future. No matter what it took, I had to get her out.

With that determination in mind, and keeping my eyes straight ahead, I walked past the guards and through the front doors of the manor as if I belonged there. No one stopped me. No one even cast me a second glance.

CHAPTER EIGHTEEN

Elianna

The sheer number of people in Lord Argall's ballroom made it difficult for me to breathe. I held
onto Zoe's arm as we entered, with guards lining the
inside of the room just as they had outside. Dozens
of human women were scattered throughout the
space—some sitting on the laps of fae males, others
mingling in the crowd. A four-piece band played on
a stage in the back of the room, with males playing
a hurdy-gurdy, a lute, drums, and a dulcian. The
upbeat music encouraged people to flock to the
dance floor. Many human women danced as part-
ners, their gorgeous ball gowns fluttering around
their ankles while intricate masks concealed their
identities. I scanned the room for Lauren and Jenny,
but with all the masked faces, it was nearly impossible to identify them without getting closer.

A guard approached me and Zoe, leading us further
into the room. "Lord Argall says you are to mingle
with the visiting males. Show them a good time.
Give them a reason to want to take you back home
with them. He left a warning for the females who
receive any complaints, so don't test him. Just do
what's expected." He tipped his chin toward the
other guards in the room. "Visiting guards can re-

quest your entertainment if they have enough coin. Lord Argall gives nothing for free." After that, he walked away before we could respond, leaving Zoe and me standing alone at the edge of the dance floor.

"I love how the guard said Lord Argall gives nothing for free when he isn't the one giving these males a damn thing," Zoe shouted, though thankfully the music drowned her out. I huffed in agreement, but the guard's words made me feel nauseous. "What's your key doing right now, Elianna? Is it still pulsing?" Her whisper in my ear was a relief; I was too close to being rescued by my mate to be caught now.

Nodding, I pulled on Zoe's arm to lead us into a darkened corner of the room. Once we were there, Zoe kept watch while I knelt down and removed the magical object from my shoe. It was pulsing and lighting up like a miniature strobe light. I quickly slid it into the pocket of my cloak, the thick fabric concealing it. "He must be nearby because it's going crazy," I said, trembling beside my friend. I couldn't tell if I was nervous or excited—probably a mix of both. "So, what do I do, Zoe?"

I scanned the room, my heart pounding with anxiety. The sheer number of men in the ballroom made finding my mate nearly impossible. He could be any one of them, but I certainly couldn't just call out for him—that would undoubtedly end badly for us both. When Zoe turned to me with a mischievous glint in her eye, I couldn't help but grin. "What?" I asked, trying to mask my unease.

"We're supposed to mingle, right?"

"Right."

"Then let's mingle. We can stay together for protection and walk past every male here. We'll start around the perimeter and then move to the dance floor, and then the eating area, if you haven't found him by then."

It seemed like a simple enough plan, but it was our best option. "How will I know when I've found him?" I asked.

Zoe arched an eyebrow, a smirk playing on her lips. "Well, I'd like to think that when you see him, you'll just know. We'll stroll at a leisurely pace, and you need to pay close attention to your key. The closer you are to him, the more the key will respond to its twin. If you don't recognize him, the magical object in your pocket will."

Nodding, I hooked my arm in Zoe's, and we sauntered toward the nearest row of guards, who were dressed in midnight blue uniforms. "The blue uniforms represent the Court of Harmony," Zoe whispered as we slowed our steps, approaching the first of the guards. Their uniforms were finely made, accented with gold buttons. Most of the males against the wall stood at attention, while some chatted with one another. Like the other partygoers, the males in uniform also wore masks, though their helmets hung from their hands. "Some of these fae males are gorgeous. Damn," Zoe remarked.

Zoe's commentary made it nearly impossible for me to suppress a giggle. I would miss my friend when I left, and the sadness that thought brought dampened my excitement. "Some of them definitely are," I replied.

For the next several minutes, we continued to creep past a line of male guards in blue—at least a dozen of them—smiling sweetly as we walked by, but my key's steady strum didn't change. It didn't intensify.

"I don't know about you," Zoe said, tugging my arm and pulling me toward the refreshment table. "If we're going to keep wandering past sexy males all night, I'm going to need a drink first." I didn't object and gladly accepted a small glass of wine before we returned to where we had left off.

Continuing our path in front of the guards from the Court of Harmony, my cheeks heated as Zoe swooned over every other one. "You'd think I'd have no interest in males after working in the brothel," she said, "but these are not the caliber of males we get there. I'm not interested in being forced to be with someone I didn't choose for myself, but I am definitely interested in having the ability to pick a mate on my own."

"And what if your mate ever shows up?" I asked.

Zoe stopped and turned to face me. "If he shows up for me, then I'll choose him. No question," she replied, shrugging. Then, as we began walking again, she added, "Well, unless he's a jerk."

I failed to stifle my laughter and covered my face with my hand, which only encouraged my friend further.

"Why are you laughing, Elianna? You'd better hope your guy isn't a jerk!" Zoe exclaimed.

I laughed harder, even as one of Lord Argall's guards shushed me. "Yes, Zoe. I hope my guy isn't a jerk."

Sipping on our wine, we meandered around the ballroom, passing in front of the green uniforms of the Court of Courage and the golden uniforms of the Court of Knowledge, where we were currently situated. As we began giggling about the names of the courts and how we imagined they had been chosen, I realized just how much stronger fae wine was compared to human wine. I wasn't drunk, but I was certainly a lot more relaxed than I had been when we entered the ballroom.

Suddenly, a large fae male—his shirt buttons straining to contain his round belly—grabbed my hand as we passed, pulling me onto his lap. I shrieked, but there was nothing I could do as his fat, pale fingers slid onto my thigh. Nearby, Zoe was helpless as another male, thinner and younger than the one who'd grabbed me, pulled her into his lap. My breaths became short, leaving me feeling lightheaded.

"Now, where were you two off to?" the rotund male asked, lighting a cigar and puffing smoke into my face. As someone who had barely survived lung cancer, I didn't appreciate it one bit, but I couldn't say anything. He smiled at me, his prominent jowls making him look like a bulldog. "What's your name, Little One?"

Smoke continued to billow in my face, forcing me to fight back the urge to gag. "Anna," I lied, purposefully. Maybe, if he didn't know my actual name, he wouldn't be able to ask the lord to purchase me, but I knew it was probably a terrible decision to lie at all.

Holding my breath, I waited for him to respond while trying to shield myself from the assault of his smoke, as well as any threat he posed. The hardness pressing against my bottom made it clear what he wanted from me if he got the chance, but I intended to ensure he would never have that chance. I was determined to escape that night, no matter what the cost.

With so many yellowed teeth, his grin made me feel a bit nauseous. "That's a beautiful name, Little One. Perfect for a tiny thing like you. How about you and your lovely friend grab me and Lord Leotris something to drink, along with a plate of food?"

I nodded and tried to rise from his lap, but his hand gripped my thigh tightly, pulling me closer and grinding his hips against me. Fear paralyzed me as I waited for him to release me. "If you're a good girl, I've got a present for you when you return."

I doubted we would agree on what constituted be-ing good or what an acceptable present was, but

I didn't argue. When I attempted to stand again, he let me go but squeezed my backside roughly as I walked away. I couldn't hear the interaction between Zoe and the male who had pulled her onto his lap, but I was relieved when my friend caught up behind me.

As soon as we were out of sight, I ducked behind a large potted plant and broke down, tears pouring out of me like a broken dam. Zoe wrapped her arm around me and pulled me into a hug. "I'm so sorry that happened to you, Elianna."

I shook my head, already aware that my friend had frequently experienced similar situations during her work at the brothel. "Do you ever get used to it? To that kind of treatment?"

"Some do, but others don't. I guess you become accustomed to expecting it, so you aren't surprised when it happens, but that doesn't make it any less uncomfortable, especially when the males are as disgusting as those were."

Squeezing my friend gently, I calmed my emotions and wiped my eyes with my cloak. "I need to find my mate, Zoe. I need to find him soon. But they're expecting us to go back."

"Then let's walk a bit more before we grab their drinks. Maybe we'll get lucky and find him, so you can escape. I'll come up with some excuse if you don't return with me."

My blood chilled, and I shook my head again. "No,

Zoe... listen. If you go back without me, they'll take it out on you if I don't return. You need to come with me. My mate can get us both out."

Noticing my friend shaking her head, I continued pleading with her. "Don't argue with me, Zoe. Please. Don't make me leave without you. We'll come back for the others; I promise you. We will come back for them. Once we're out, we can find somewhere safe, hopefully locate your mate, and then gather support to return and rescue the women."

"Elianna, I need my key to find my mate. I don't have it, and I have no way to get it."

A thought struck me, filling my eyes with hope. "Zoe, do you know how to get in touch with Pith?"

"Why? What exactly would we need a grumpy, mumbling little creature for right now?"

I grabbed both of Zoe's hands to make her look into my eyes, my hope expanding in the shadowed spaces inside me. "It was Pith who found my key and gave it to Hiedra so she could pass it on to me. If we can get Pith, he can get your key. He grabbed mine and returned in an instant."

Zoe bit her lip, looking contemplative. "If we can safely get my key back, then I'll leave with you. We'll need to go somewhere private to get his attention—maybe the library since it's close to the ballroom."

That was all I needed to hear. I grabbed my friend's hand and practically ran out from behind the plant where we'd been hiding. I was moving so quickly that I didn't notice the tall, broad-shouldered male in a crimson uniform barreling straight toward me.

I halted as he almost ran me over. He muttered an apology before continuing in front of me, tendrils of his dark, shoulder-length hair slipping from the leather tie at his neck. With the golden mask on his face, all I could make out in that moment when our eyes met was that his golden eyes were rimmed in dark green. His eyes were beautiful—unique and entrancing. They made me want to chase after him, if only to admire them a little longer. My key must have felt the same way, because the moment my heart calmed from our brief interaction, the enchanted object in my pocket pulsed with an intensified fury I'd never seen before. The male with the beautiful eyes was my mate.

CHAPTER NINETEEN

Blaze

A human female darted out from a shadowed area near the wall, almost knocking me over. She caught me by surprise as I headed toward where the soldiers in crimson were instructed to stand. I turned to apologize, but I was captivated by the blue eyes peeking out from behind the golden mask that covered her delicate face. Even with her short, chestnut hair, she was beautiful, but I turned away. I needed to find my mate, and I couldn't risk getting kicked out of the ballroom for being in the wrong place or wasting my time talking to another female.

It was only after I turned back and began walking away that I realized something was happening; my body seemed to tremble. My key was reacting to either her or the female on her arm. I struggled to breathe at the realization, but when I turned around, she stood just a foot away, her eyes bright as she stared at me.

With my heart racing, I stepped forward to close the distance between us. She remained still, her breath hitching as her lips parted slightly. Time stood still as I gazed at her. She was everything I had ever dreamed of.

As discreetly as possible, I pulled the key from my pocket, careful to hold it just inside my cloak to conceal its persistent glow. Her breath hitched at the sight of it, and realization widened her eyes. "Are you mine?" I whispered. I knew she heard me when she slipped her hand inside her own cloak and pulled out a flashing golden key—my key's twin.

"If you're mine," she responded.

The attraction between our keys was magnetic, their magical halves combining to form a whole. We watched the enchanted objects connect, the flickering lights dimming as the magic settled. Emotions flooded me. I wanted to wrap my arms around her, to kiss her, but I couldn't—not in the middle of a ballroom filled with men eager to buy and use her. I scanned the area to ensure no one had witnessed our interaction before returning my gaze to my mate.

"I have to get you out of here," I said, my voice barely above a whisper. She nodded, and her friend linked their arms together once more.

The two women followed me as I made my way toward the door. My anxiety heightened with every step, but I had a plan. The guards were instructed to take women to their beds if they had enough coin to pay for their services. With the amount of money I had, including some I had taken from a coin purse left carelessly among some gear in the hallway, I had enough to secure my mate and her friend for an hour. That was all I needed; by the end of that hour, I would have them off the lord's property and on their way to freedom. I wouldn't be bringing them back. All I needed to do was get them out of the ballroom, and I was confident I could get them off the grounds and onto Shadow's back before anyone became suspicious.

I glanced back at my mate before approaching the guard I needed to pay. As quickly as she was breathing, I could tell she was panicking, and I hated how stressful the situation had been for her. All I wanted at that moment was to get her somewhere safe and hold her in my arms. When I grinned at her over my shoulder, she blushed, sending flutters through my stomach. The feelings she was already stirring in me were like nothing I'd ever experienced before, and I couldn't wait to feel them again.

The guard at the door was clad in black, one of Lord Argall's men, as I soon realized. I pulled two silver coins from my pouch and handed them to the guard. "For the hour," I said, praying to Solstice that the guard wouldn't raise any objections.

To my relief, the guard nodded. "You can have them for one hour, but if they return with visible wounds or bruises, if they come back dirty or with torn clothes, or if they don't come back at all, your head will end up on a pike by the front gates. Those are Lord Argall's rules. Do you accept these conditions?"

They wouldn't be coming back at all, and I knew

my head wouldn't end up on a pike, but I voiced my acceptance before guiding the two women out of the ballroom and into the hallway. Once there, I turned down another corridor and pulled my mate into my arms. The scent that filled my nose felt familiar and comforting, like one I'd known and loved my entire life. When I pulled away to look into her eyes, they were glassy, threatening tears. "What's your name? Mine's Blaze."

The smile that spread across her perfect face nearly made me melt. "Elianna. My friend is Zoe. If you're rescuing me, I'm rescuing her."

It would complicate the escape, but I had no intention of disappointing her or breaking her heart, so I nodded. "I'm going to rescue both of you, but is there anything you need before we leave? The sooner we get off this property, the better our chances of avoiding capture."

Zoe, my mate's blond-haired friend, chewed on her bottom lip nervously before speaking. "We need to go to the library so I can summon the brownie who cleans our room. There's something we can't leave without."

Wrapping my arm around Elianna's tiny waist, I nodded in acknowledgment. "Lead the way."

Zoe cautiously moved forward, scanning our surroundings before turning down another corridor that appeared to lead deeper into the house. I followed closely with Elianna still in my arms. We passed only a few closed doorways before Zoe walked through a set of wooden doors into a darkened library. Quietly, I closed the door behind us.

The library was massive and was empty, but a few lanterns glowed throughout the space. Zoe approached one of the lit areas, muttering a few words before snapping her fingers. Almost immediately, a brownie appeared. Having grown up in Ecromos, I was familiar with these tiny creatures, both their unfortunate appearances and their unpleasant personalities. I listened as the women spoke to the brownie, keeping my eyes peeled for any signs of movement in the library. If we got caught in there, my head would definitely end up on a pike.

After speaking with Elianna and her friend, the brownie vanished, but only for a short while before reappearing and handing satchels to the two females. The last item the brownie gave to Zoe before it disappeared was something wrapped in a black cloth. When she unwrapped it, I understood why contacting the brownie had been so crucial; inside the fabric was a key. It illuminated when she touched it, pulling a gasp from her lips before she tightly wrapped it back up and slipped it into her pocket.

Once the creature vanished again, the two women approached me, eagerness evident on their faces. "We're ready now," Elianna said, smiling.

"Good. Do either of you know if there's a way to exit the manor from here?" I asked.

Elianna nodded enthusiastically. "Pith just told us that there's a hidden door behind one of the tapestries."

I found myself getting lost in her big blue eyes as she spoke, captivated by how they sparkled when she smiled. Forcing myself back to the present, I took her hand, feeling the softness of her skin against mine. "Let's go."

Taking the lantern from the table, the blonde female walked toward the back wall of the library, weaving through the stacks that filled the space. Once concealed, Elianna and her friend quickly slipped out of their gowns. They dropped them on the library floor, donning tunics and trousers from the bags given to them by the brownie. I kept watch, relieved not to see any movement in the vast, cavernous area.

There were several tapestries on the wall, and it wasn't until we searched behind the fourth one that we found the hidden door.

The corridor beyond the doorway was dark, the single lantern providing little illumination. The air was humid, carrying the musty scent of mold. I pulled my sword from its scabbard and took the lead, with my mate holding onto the back of my cloak. I had given both women a dagger before we entered the passage, hoping they would know how to use them if the situation arose.

We crept forward, moving silently to avoid alerting anyone to our presence. The corridor stretched out before us; it was not just a simple door leading to the back of the structure. By the time we reached the exit door, the women had already been with me for nearly thirty minutes, leaving me only a limited time to get them as far away from the manor as possible before the guards realized they hadn't been returned.

I lowered the lantern's flame until it was nearly extinguished and nudged the door open just enough to peer outside. To my relief, the corridor opened to the side yard of the house, which wasn't guarded, as no one was supposed to be using it. There were guards nearby, but those remaining outside, instead of joining the party, were gathered around scattered fires, drinking and chatting. No one seemed to be paying attention to where we were, at least from what I could see.

"I'm going to turn off the lantern completely. When I open this door, we'll walk quickly but silently toward those trees. My horse is waiting there. Once we reach the woods, we'll talk again. Are both of you ready to go?"

Once they nodded, I lowered the lantern's flame. A moment later, I kissed my mate on the cheek, bringing a flush to her skin. Then, I opened the door, and the three of us stepped outside.

Just as I had instructed, the two women walked quickly but quietly, following behind me as I led them into the forest where Shadow was supposed to be. No one appeared to have seen us, but there was no guarantee of that. Still, I couldn't worry about that at the moment; we needed to keep moving.

Once we were fully immersed in the forest, I let out a quick whistle. The sound of Shadow's footfalls reached my keen fae ears only a heartbeat later. When the horse got close enough, I placed our packs into the saddlebags. With their supplies secured, I lifted Zoe and then Elianna onto the saddle before climbing on behind them. Thankfully, both women were petite, and my horse was massive, or we wouldn't have all fit on her back.

Using my boots, I nudged Shadow into a silent walk, bringing us further into the forest. To avoid being seen, my goal was to travel along the perimeter of the property through the woods, exiting the tree cover only once we reached the gate. Since there was less brush near the stone walls, Shadow picked up to a trot.

By the time we arrived at the gate, everything had gone smoothly. I still heard distant talking around the fires, but none of the voices were near us. There were no guards at the gate; the party was more enticing than standing outside in the cold, dark night. It wouldn't have surprised me if they had abandoned their posts to mingle with the women indoors, their negligence making it easier for me to sneak the women off the property.

"Put your hoods up and lean back into me. From a distance, we want it to look like there's only one person on this horse, and no more than two," I instructed.

Nodding in agreement, they followed my directions, pulling their hooded cloaks tightly around themselves. With Zoe nestled against her chest, Elianna leaned back against me, the warmth of her body sending a rush of heat through my blood. I slipped my arm around her waist, trying my best to keep my focus on our escape as I maneuvered Shadow forward, out of the tree line, and through the open gate.

CHAPTER TWENTY

Elianna

My fated mate had come for me. This realization continued to swirl through my mind as we rode away from Lord Argall's property, my prison, and onto the dirt road that would lead us to freedom. My heart thundered with excitement as Blaze's arm wrapped around my waist, anchoring me to safety. Zoe leaned into my chest, her mere presence filling me with even more relief. I had never expected to escape the manor, so getting my friend out as well was something I had only ever dreamed about.

I had spent months wondering about the person who had the twin to my key. What did he look like? Would he be a good person? Would I be attracted to him? So many questions flooded my mind, especially when I settled into bed at night. But I could have never created Blaze in my wildest imagination. With deep brown hair falling to his shoulders and the warmth of his golden eyes, rimmed in the darkest shade of green, Blaze was ruggedly handsome. His face exuded masculine strength, from his strong jawline and straight nose to the dark stubble that gave him a bit of a five o'clock shadow, only making him more attractive.

I had dated a few boys in the past, although dating is a weak term for it since cancer had limited my experiences. But Blaze was a man—well, not exactly a man, but an adult fae male.

The thought of being alone with him for the first time made me shiver. I imagined how he would know exactly how to touch me. As Lord Argall claimed, I was pure, a virgin. The most I had ever done with a guy was share a kiss. I was nervous yet excited about experiencing the things I had missed with someone so special. Although I didn't know him well, we had been chosen for each other by fate, creating a bond we couldn't deny. In human terms, he was already my husband, my forever, so I wouldn't hold back, not if he treated me well. He had already proven his love for me by putting his life at risk while rescuing my best friend and me, earning his place by my side.

The horse beneath us galloped down the dirt road for a short while before darting into the forest. Sandwiched between Zoe and Blaze, I barely had room to move, but I felt safe. I tried to watch the forest as we passed, the area quiet except for the occasional sounds made by animals, but with the moon only a sliver in the sky, its light barely reached the forest floor. The darkness would aid in keeping us hidden, but it also concealed potential dangers.

"I know you must both be tired," Blaze said, leaning over my back, his warm breath against my ear making my stomach tingle. "But we need to get farther from Cloudfell before we stop to rest." His words echoed the exhaustion we all felt, the weight of our journey pressing down on us.

Sliding my arm across the one he had draped over my stomach, I intertwined my fingers with his. "Do you know of somewhere safe where we can sleep?"

"I'm afraid nowhere in the Court of Knowledge will be completely safe, my Starlight," he replied. "But there is a campsite I'm aiming for. If my companions are there, it will be even safer."

Still, Starlight. The pet name caught me by surprise, but I liked it. The thought of joining other males I didn't know filled me with uncertainty, but that feeling passed quickly. After everything Blaze had done to save me, I knew he would never intentionally put me in harm's way. Although I had my trust issues, I realized I could trust him.

"Who are they? The other males. Are they your family?" I asked.

Leaning forward, he tucked a tendril of his short hair behind my ear. "Not by blood, but I do consider them family. We rode a long way together and faced dangers together. We parted ways because I needed to find you, and they needed medication for one of their sick children. It's an older father and his two adult sons. They're good males, so don't worry." He kissed me on the cheek, his soft lips lingering for a moment, as though he didn't want to pull away. "We agreed to meet back at our last campsite after I found you because the forest is a dangerous place to traverse. We'll be heading in the same direction. Having three more males who can wield weapons will keep you and Zoe much safer than I can alone. Hopefully, they're already there waiting for us. Either way, we won't be able to stay in one place for too long, since the lord probably already knows that the two of you are missing and is sending out guards to find us."

A familiar heaviness settled in my chest. We'd escaped and had come so far already. I couldn't bear the thought of being recaptured; it was too horrifying.

Shadow's steps slowed as the brush became thicker, with coiling vines and bushes making our path difficult to navigate. I leaned back into Blaze, tucking my head beneath his chin as he held onto the reins. It took me a moment to realize that Zoe had fallen asleep against me. Her hood covered her eyes, making it hard to tell whether they were closed. I wrapped my arms around her tightly, not wanting her to fall.

"Is she sleeping?" Blaze asked, keeping his voice low as he peeked over my head. I nodded. I knew he didn't want to stop yet, but I didn't want Zoe to fall off the horse either. We were still too close to the lord's manor. Still, we needed to find somewhere safe to stay because we were all exhausted.

"Change of plans. Just for tonight, we'll go deeper into the forest, but we can try to find a safe place to rest. My friends were not planning to meet me at the other location for three more days, so we have time. If we can find a secure location, perhaps we can stay there for a few days at least until we meet up with Baltair and his sons. By the time those three days are up, if the lord hasn't found us, maybe he'll think we're too far away to continue pursuing us. It's a good hope, anyway."

The thought lifted some of the worry from my chest. "Do you think that could happen? That he'll give up?"

"I don't know if he'll give up, but he may not know where to look if he thinks we're long gone." His mouth slid away from my ear as he placed a gentle kiss on my neck. The sensation of his breath and lips against my skin made something tighten in my lower belly. It was like he couldn't help but touch me, and I loved it. "Do you want to go with that plan?"

The intimate touches to my neck had my head in a tizzy, and our conversation was no longer my first focus. "Huh?"

He chuckled, clearly realizing the effect he had on me. "I asked if you wanted to find a safe place to rest before continuing on."

Heat colored my cheeks, and I was grateful it was dark outside. "Yes. Let's do that. Your kisses are—um—distracting me."

"Is that so, my Starlight?" He leaned forward again, nuzzling his face into my neck. The touch was electric, sensations I had never felt before surging through my body. I closed my eyes as his nose glided along the sensitive flesh between my neck and shoulder, trailing back with his tongue. The sensation of his warm, wet tongue sliding across my skin made me feel molten, desire heating my core.

Words were struggling to find their way out as I gasped for breath. "I think we really need to find a place to—*uh*—rest. Soon."

I realized I probably sounded like a desperate, lustful woman, something I had never been before, but I didn't care. There were no expectations for us to move at a certain pace, even though we were fated mates. But I wanted him, needed him. If he would have me, I would give myself to him.

After traveling several more miles into the dark woods, we stumbled across an abandoned cabin just as the sky turned pink with the blooming sunrise. We rode the perimeter, ensuring there were no other travelers nearby, before dismounting and returning to the small stone cabin. After settling Shadow near a large patch of grass, Blaze entered the cabin first with his sword in hand, checking to make sure it was empty. It appeared to have been abandoned for a long time. Once he deemed it safe, Zoe, who had only just woken up, and I entered the stone structure, with Blaze following behind.

The cabin had only a single bedroom and bathroom, aside from the modest living area and kitchen. It was just as small as it appeared from the

outside. There was no running water or the com-
forts we were used to, but it was isolated enough to
provide us shelter while we rested.

Zoe and I stayed near the cabin, collecting fire-
wood and hauling it to the fireplaces, while Blaze
filled buckets with water from the pump outside.
Thanks to the meager food Pith had taken from the
kitchens and placed in our bags, we didn't need to
search for food yet. He may have been a grumpy
little creature, but Pith had been a lifesaver with
the items he had stuffed into the satchels before we
fled.

The inside of the cabin was dirty, with vines growing up the outside of the building and creeping
across the walls inside. Zoe and I did our best to
clean the floors, at least enough to make it tolerable.
There was no mattress in the bedroom, nor was
there any comfortable furniture in the living area,
but at least we had a few blankets. We cleaned as
Blaze started fires in both rooms and boiled water
for tea and bathing.

By the time we settled in front of the fire in the
living area to eat, we were filthy and exhausted. Zoe
cleaned up first, opting to use a rag to wash herself
instead of filling the tub. Once she had put on a
clean set of clothes from her satchel, she lay on a
bedroll near the fire and fell asleep.

As I cleaned myself up, Blaze checked on Shadow,
bringing the horse into the small stable attached
to the cabin before returning inside and securing

the door. We could only do so much to ensure our safety; others were undoubtedly looking for us, but the cabin would have to suffice for the day.

Once Blaze finished double-checking every lock and securing the threadbare curtains over the windows, he went into the bedroom and removed the crimson Court of Chaos jacket and shirt, tossing them into the fire. I watched him from the blanket pallet on the floor, my mouth going dry as my eyes traced the details of his muscular body and how his long hair fell in loose waves after being freed from its strap. He stood in front of the fire for a moment, a contemplative expression on his face as the uniform burned.

When he turned to look at me, his eyes reflected the same relief and awe I felt. In that moment, I knew without a doubt that being with him was exactly where I was meant to be, no matter how much we had endured to be together. Now that I had him, I never intended to let him go.

CHAPTER
TWENTY-ONE

Blaze

After patrolling the area around the cabin twice, both on horseback and on foot, I was satisfied that we would be safe there, at least for the night. While collecting water, I had set a simple trap in the brush—one to catch a meal and another to slow down any unwanted visitors. Upon re-entering the cabin and checking the locks on the doors and windows, I threw the uniform of my former enemy into the fire. It burned quickly, the crimson fabric turning into nothing more than crimson flames.

Zoe, the blond female, had fallen back asleep on the floor of the living area near the fire. Due to our need for silence during the escape, she had said little. With no mate to claim her, I realized that Elianna's friend would be with us for the foreseeable future. However, I had noticed the way her key flickered when she unwrapped it, which led me to wonder if her mate was looking for her while we hid inside the abandoned cabin. If he came for her, we had to be ready.

As I turned away from the fire, my mind racing with

thoughts, I spotted Elianna. After days of searching and worrying, she was finally there, and she looked perfect. I couldn't take my eyes off my new mate. She had just finished washing up when I walked in, sitting in the lantern light, dressed only in a tunic, her breasts pressing against the thin fabric. I was overwhelmed with desire. We hadn't yet discussed going to bed together, but I could smell her arousal when I kissed her neck. I would never pressure her into anything she wasn't ready for, but the way she looked at me, heavy-lidded, as I took off my shirt and washed myself, told me that if I made a move, she would welcome it.

Adding another log to the fire, I crossed the room, her gaze never leaving me as I lowered myself onto the floor next to her, leaving my trousers on. "I guess there's a lot we need to learn about each other," I said.

She smiled, a flush creeping into her cheeks that stirred something inside my chest that had been quiet for too long. "We do." As she tucked her hair behind her ear, I couldn't help but admire the delicately rounded tip of her ear, so different from my own. "Thank you for rescuing me... I don't know what I would have done if you hadn't found me."

A tear slipped down her cheek, and I gently wiped it away with my thumb as I cupped her face in my hand. For a moment, we gazed at each other, as if we couldn't believe the other was real. Fate had brought us together, even though we had come from entirely different worlds. The significance of that moment wasn't lost on me, nor on her. "Don't cry, my Starlight," I whispered. "I would have never given up on finding you. But we're together now. You're safe."

She nodded, leaning into my touch, her eyes fluttering closed as I stroked her cheek. When she opened her eyes again, the fear had vanished. The fire crackled, and the warmth from the flames made the drafty cabin feel cozier. I couldn't wait to take her home and start our lives together. There was so much I wanted to tell her and ask her, but that could all come in time. After all, we had our entire lives to learn everything there was to know about each other, so we didn't need to unpack it all in one night.

The one thing I couldn't wait another moment to do was kiss her, for her exquisite mouth drew me in. She didn't break my gaze as I closed the distance between us. Instead, she leaned forward, her lips grazing mine in the softest of touches, sending a jolt of electricity through me at the first contact. It took everything in me to pull away, to search her face for any sign that I had moved too quickly. But the flush on her cheeks, the shy smile on her face, and the way she reached up to slide her fingers through my hair, pulling me back into another kiss, put all my concerns to rest.

Wrapping my arm around her waist, I pulled Elianna onto my lap, her body feeling so much smaller than mine. Her hands gripped the back of my neck as I held her close, pulling her even nearer. Tilting her head back, I slid my tongue along the seam of her lips, and she opened for me, deepening the kiss. I groaned; the taste of her against my tongue was sublime. The mating bond, the attraction drawing us together like a moth to a flame—it was everything. It was love. It was life. It was forever.

With her hands on my shoulders, she pushed me until I was lying on my back atop the jumble of blankets, her legs straddling me. She never broke our kiss as she leaned down over me.

"I want you, Blaze," she said, her voice low and breathy. The desperation in her tone hit me hard. I clenched my teeth, fighting against my body's desire as much as hers.

When Elianna moved to lift her tunic over her head, I placed a hand on her forearm to stop her. "We don't have to rush," I said. She started to object, but I took her hand and brought it to my lips, kissing it. Her mouth closed as she watched me. "I want you more than anything I've ever wanted in my life, but today has been an emotionally charged day for both of us. When we make love, I want it to be on a soft bed, not on a dirty floor. I want you to feel safe, and to know that you'll still be safe tomorrow."

Taking her hands, which were laid across my bare stomach, I pulled her back down against me and kissed the top of her head. She nuzzled into my neck, and the wisp of her breath against my skin only made everything feel more sensitive, making my decision to wait all the more difficult. "But if you're ready, when we find that safe place with a soft bed, I'm going to kiss every part of your body. I'm going to show you how much you mean to me; I will worship you like the goddess you are. We're going to take our time, and after we share ecstasy together, I'll hold you in that soft bed all night. I promise. It will be worth waiting for."

After I finished speaking and kissed her head again, my hand running lazy strokes across her back, she kissed me back, her touch slow and sensual. It wasn't long before her breathing evened out, and her chest rose and fell in a gentle rhythm as she fell asleep on top of me. Before I'd found her, I had told myself I wouldn't get a full night of sleep until my mate was safely in my arms. Now that she was sleeping peacefully, her face in my mind and the taste of her on my lips, I finally drifted off to sleep.

When I awoke the next morning, with Elianna in my arms, it was the happiest and most well-rested I had felt upon waking in as long as I could remember. I knew our challenges were not over. We were still on the run, and until we escaped the reach of Lord Argall—where he couldn't find her and Zoe—we would remain in danger. That's why, as I lay there with my mate still sleeping soundly, I decided to stick to the plan of staying in the abandoned cabin for one more day. If the nobles were searching for us, I doubted they would still be combing the forests near Cloudfell. They would likely expect us to have fled the city without stopping, riding as far away and as quickly as possible. Given my chances of outrunning guards on horseback, and considering my group was tired, I felt it was safest and smartest to hide out for a few days and let the search parties either move on or give up.

Through the doorway separating the small bed-chamber from the living area, I could just make out Zoe's frame in the dark as she piled more logs on the fire. The sound of her striking kindling made Elianna stir against me. Her blue eyes shone as she opened them and saw me lying beside her.

She smiled, her face delicate and magnificent like a spring flower. "Good morning," she said, rubbing her eyes.

Something in my chest fluttered at her smile. It must have been what love felt like, I thought. It was like the magic in our keys, the same magic that made us fated for each other, had also planted us in one another's hearts and souls, so the love and connection could grow before we ever met. It was a beautiful and exciting revelation, and I couldn't help but smile back at her before leaning forward to place a lingering kiss on her lips. "Good morning to you, my Starlight."

"Is Zoe up yet?" she asked, glancing over her shoulder, though she couldn't see her friend from that angle. I flicked my gaze in the same direction. Having started the fire, Zoe hung a cauldron over the flames to boil water.

"She is. I believe she just woke up a little while ago."

Even knowing her friend was awake, Elianna seemed in no hurry to leave the warmth of the blankets. "What's our plan for today? Assuming we won't be finding a soft bed...?" Her grin was mischievous, pulling a chuckle from me. I was starting to think my new mate was a bit feistier than I had realized—perhaps even more than she knew. It warmed my heart to know that she hadn't wanted me the night before only because her emotions were in overdrive, but that she genuinely wanted me even after waking with a clear mind. It was hard to refrain when she was so willing, but I would because taking her on the dirty floor wouldn't show her the respect she deserved. I hated that she had to sleep there, but it was only temporary.

I ran my hand up and down her arm, eliciting a shiver from her as tiny goosebumps raised on her skin. "If you want that soft bed, I'll make it my mission to find one for you as soon as I can. I live to please you. But for today, we will stay here and hide. Hopefully, by the end of the day, the searchers will have moved on or given up. I'm going to check on Shadow and my traps, so hopefully, we'll have a fresh meal."

She nodded, kissing me again before pushing herself up to sit. "Then I'll dig through our rations to fix something for us to eat and check on Zoe."

CHAPTER
TWENTY-TWO

Elianna

When Blaze left the cabin, I quickly pulled on a pair of trousers and boots before heading out to the living area to see Zoe. I felt relieved that we had been able to meet with Pith before leaving the manor; traveling on horseback in a gown would have been a nightmare, especially since the sparkling fabric would have made us obvious targets.

Sitting on the floor with her long legs stretched out before her, Zoe sipped from a mug of tea. "Good morning," she said with a genuine smile as I entered the room.

"Morning to you. How did you sleep?" I asked.

Zoe yawned. "You know, even though I slept on the floor, I still slept better than I have in a long time. I think it's easier to rest when you're free than when you're a slave."

With Blaze by my side, holding me as I slept, I realized I was having a much different experience than my friend. I wondered about Zoe's mate. Now that she had her key back, the metal object flickering in her hand, he could show up at any time.

"So..." Zoe stretched the word. "Blaze is quite handsome. Are you going to share any of the juicy details with me, or do I have to beg?"

I couldn't hide the flush on my cheeks, but Blaze's entrance back into the cabin spared me from having to explain.

Glancing from my reddened cheeks to Zoe's curious gaze, Blaze wore a purely mischievous smirk. "I've interrupted something good, haven't I?"

Zoe snickered and twisted the golden key in her hand, which flashed back at her. "I think I like him, Elianna."

Then Blaze blushed as he lowered himself to the floor next to me. "The perimeter looks good. There were no signs of anyone besides animals. I reset my traps so I can catch dinner."

"I take that back, Elianna. I may love him," Zoe said, scooting across the floor to try to squish herself between us. "You can find another mate."

Blaze chuckled as he pulled me onto his lap while Zoe moved back to her spot, the key still twisting in her hand. Being on Blaze's lap reminded me of our night together, how good it felt to be close to him, and how close we had come to being completely together. My body warmed to his touch, and butterflies filled my stomach.

"By how the metal responds to your closeness, I'd say your mate is out there looking for you," Blaze said, his calloused hand stroking my back. "He may take a while to find you, but he still has the twin in his possession. It wouldn't be so active if he didn't."

Zoe's eyes lit up at Blaze's words. "I hope you're right."

We spent the entire day inside the cabin, gathered around the fire, resting, talking, and cooking the rabbit that Blaze had caught in the trap he set that morning. Blaze occasionally patrolled the property, never straying far, fearing that someone might be hiding nearby, waiting for the chance to capture us and take us back to Lord Argall. I still hadn't told my new mate about my recently discovered powers. I didn't fully understand them myself, and it never felt like the right time to bring it up.

As the sun set on our second night in the cabin, Blaze decided we would leave the following day for the campsite, where he planned to meet the father and sons he had mentioned. Although Lord Argall could still have guards searching the area, we couldn't stay in the cabin indefinitely, and the forest was dense. If we stayed off the main roads, as we intended, we hoped to remain undetected.

There was still no sign of Zoe's mate, although her key continued to respond to her touch. When we were still inside the manor, she had lost all hope of ever finding the male she was destined for, but I could see the yearning in my friend's eyes when she held the enchanted object in her hands, feeling its surge of power. After finding my own mate, I remained hopeful that she would do the same. After everything she had been through, Zoe deserved happiness.

After we ate, Blaze brought in more water for the bath, warming it over the fire. Once Zoe finished cleaning and settled down to sleep by the fire in the living area, he prepared a fresh pot of clean water for both himself and me. It was hard to fully unwind in the bath, not while we felt so unsettled and were in the dusty old cabin, so I cleaned quickly while Blaze checked on Shadow. When he returned to the cabin a short time later, I was already sitting on our makeshift bed, waiting for him.

He grinned at me, and I lifted my lip in response. Untying the straps on his tunic, Blaze kept his eyes on me a moment longer. I nibbled on my lower lip, though all I really wanted was to stand up and nibble on him. He had told me we wouldn't make love until we had a proper bed, but the mating bond between us made it difficult to wait.

"Are you tired?" he asked as he stepped toward me,

bending down to kiss the top of my head.

When he turned to walk away to the bathing room, I gripped his trousers, tugging him back. "I don't think I could sleep just yet."

Blaze turned to me, a wicked smile on his face as he looked into my eyes. "What do you want to do, then?"

Reaching for the front of his trousers, I pulled at the ties, trying to undo them, but Blaze placed a hand over mine, stopping me. I gasped. "I know you said you wanted to wait to make love until we have a bed under us, but I just really want to touch you. Please."

The fire in Blaze's eyes smoldered, deepening the shade of gold. Crouching in front of me, he took my face in his hands and pulled me into a kiss, his tongue possessing me, none of the touches tender or hesitant. Not on this night. When he pulled away, I was panting. "Just let me get cleaned up first, because I've been cleaning out Shadow's stable and I'm quite disgusting. I'll be right back."

Nodding through lust-filled eyes, I watched as Blaze walked into the bathroom, dropping his clothes on the floor before closing the door. My jaw fell open as I tried to process what I'd just seen. Blaze's backside was perfectly sculpted, as though it had been cut from marble. His thighs were thick with muscle, the strength in his body mouthwatering. If someone had pointed him out to me before I'd met him and called him a god, I would have believed them.

I listened to the water splashing from behind the door, imagining what his abdominal muscles looked like with water dripping down them, and realized I was incredibly attracted to my mate. It was one of the big unknowns I'd worried about before leaving the human world, worrying I wouldn't be attracted to my fated mate, but that worry had been completely put to rest. There was no question how sexy I found him, how irresistible. Perhaps it was because he was handsome, or maybe it was due to the mating bond. Either way, I wanted to give him everything, every part of me I'd never given to anyone else.

When Blaze returned from the bathing room with nothing on aside from his trousers with untied laces, he walked straight to me, lowering himself onto the bedding and kissing me deeply. I wrapped my arms around his shoulders, threading my fingers through his long hair.

Leaning back onto the blankets, he pulled me on top of him, the gentle stroke of his tongue against mine never pausing, never losing the connection. My thighs framed his hips as I pulled away, lips swollen and panting. His heartbeat pounded against my chest, and his hardness twitched against the fabric of my undergarments. I ground against him, letting out a breathy moan that seemed to make him nearly lose control. His hips lifted against me.

"I want to take you, to claim you as mine." The gravel in his voice sent a shiver along my skin, settling in the deepest parts of me. "I want to worship you, and

I will, but not here."

I heard his words, and I wanted to argue, but although he didn't want to go all the way with me while in the cabin, he didn't seem to want to deny me other pleasures. Each time I ground myself against his cock, separated by only the fabric of our clothing, his grunts made me think he was close to unraveling. My release continued to build with the friction of his hardness against my center.

Instead of arguing, my mouth went to his neck, kissing his skin. He groaned, his hips bucking against the apex of my thighs as I worked myself against him, my lips leaving his neck to return to his mouth, the kiss hungry and claiming. My hips held him tight as I rode his lap. The fabric of his trousers and my undergarments separated our skin from touching, but I didn't care.

Whether it was attraction or magic that created the feverish need inside of me, I didn't know, but it was undeniable. The sounds that came out of me, the huffs, grunts, and moans, became more desperate as I moved over him, using his hardness against my softness, to drive myself to climax. It was like nothing I'd ever experienced, my lower belly twisting up like a coil with every slide against him.

Gripping my hips tightly, Blaze helped to guide my movements, lifting his hips to meet mine, increasing the friction against me. I wanted him inside of me, wanted to take our remaining clothes off, and let him claim me. He wouldn't, but I wanted him to.

"I'm so close, Blaze, but you—" My words broke off as my movements became more erratic, and I screamed, my body tensing and trembling over him, before I collapsed in a boneless, panting heap.

I lay sprawled across the top of him as his hand rubbed up and down my back, his lips placing a kiss against my temple. "This was about your pleasure. But trust me when I tell you that was the most erotic thing I've ever done, and I got plenty pleasure from it too, my Starlight." He kissed me again, his breath warm against my cheek. "And I cannot wait to get you into a soft bed, so we can do that again, but maybe with fewer clothes."

Grinning against his chest, I slid my hand between our bodies and gripped his length through his trousers, the wet spot on the fabric showing just how turned on he really was. He groaned. "I look forward to that soft bed, too. I'll also need to come up with a nickname for you."

He leaned up to look into my face, the flames in the hearth making his golden eyes appear on fire. "Do you not like your nickname?"

Blaze's grin made me giggle. My face rested on my fist. "I actually love my nickname. It reminds me of what my father called me." Just thinking about my dad brought back those feelings of loss and grief. Even though my parents were still alive, I could never see them again, which made it feel like they were already gone.

Seeming to see the change in my features, his playful features softened, and he reached up to run his fingers across my cheek, tucking my hair behind my ear. "What did your father call you?"

"Firefly."

CHAPTER TWENTY-THREE

Blaze

"When you left Master's manor, Pith didn't think he'd find you sleeping on the floor. Dusty and dirty. I refuse to clean such a dirty home, Miss Lazy Bones." I would've thought I was dreaming, but the feeling of my blanket being pulled off jolted me awake. Reaching for my blade, I rubbed the sleep from my eyes, squinting up at the creature with giant green eyes and a floppy brown hat standing on the side of our makeshift bed. The brownie I'd seen in Lord Argall's library was leaning over Elianna as she slept on the floor next to me. "You need to wake up, Lazy Bones. Unless you want Master to find you. You and your handsome friend with the nice hair need to leave now. Oh, and don't leave Miss Zoc here. I won't clean this mess for her, either."

Waking next to me, Elianna pulled the blanket up to her chin, jumping when her eyes landed on the miniature being in front of her. "Pith? What are you doing here? How did you even get here?"

I stood, tying the laces on my trousers before strapping on my weapons. Pith turned his head away from Elianna, tracking all my movements before looking back at her.

"Lazy Bones talks to Pith, so Pith wanted to find her and make her bed. This isn't a bed, though, Lazy Bones. I can't clean this one. And then I saw the horses. And then I thought Lazy Bones might be in trouble. The dirty floor, though. Lazy Bones shouldn't sleep on this."

"Pith, please try to stay on the most important topic. Why did you say the Master would find her?" I lowered myself to the brownie's height, crouching next to my mate, who was still lying in the blankets.

Pith turned to look at me, the brownie clearly exasperated. "Pith said Master will find Lazy Bones because Master is almost here with his horses. He's looking for her and Miss Zoe. Master is very angry."

Shooting up from her place on the makeshift bed, Elianna reached for her clothes, pulling them on quickly. "How close, Pith? How close is he?"

Snapping his fingers, Pith disappeared, only to reappear a moment later. "A few miles away. Master's guards are still on the road."

Darting into the living area, I told Zoe what was going on, and the female wasted no time in packing up her meager belongings and pulling on her boots. We left the cabin a moment later. I shoved our packs into the saddlebags and hoisted the two human females onto Shadow's back. With the human females draped in dark cloaks, we moved toward the south, deeper into the forest and away from the main road.

Day had just begun to break when Pith had woken us in the cabin. After assuring Elianna he would find her again, the brownie disappeared. After what he'd done for us, I owed him everything. When we settled, I fully intended to offer him a home with us. My fae ears zeroed in on the surrounding forest, listening for sounds of a cavalry, voices, or the footfalls of horses, but heard none. We traveled in silence, Shadow moving like a ghost through the trees.

Just like the forest closest to the Sanctuary of Healing, everything looked the same. With little familiarity with the Court of Knowledge, all I had to guide me was my compass. I didn't know how I would find the campsite where we were to meet Baltair and his sons, but Shadow's steps didn't falter. I may not have remembered the way, but my horse seemed to remember.

Having to detour deeper into the forest to avoid the cavalry near the main road, it took us twice as long to get to the campsite than I'd expected. We arrived back at the location around midday, and as I'd expected, the Oathorne family had yet to return. The campsite was empty, but I knew we were in the right place thanks to the marks I'd left on a few trees as we'd passed. We couldn't remain there for long, not with Lord Argall on the hunt for us, not longer than one day. I wasn't comfortable being out in the open at all. Still, everyone needed rest, and I felt even less comfortable with the idea of heading back toward my own court with the two women alone.

We dismounted Shadow but left her untethered, just in case we had to go without warning. After starting a small fire, I set up the tent, Zoe entering right away to get more rest. When I stood with my sword in hand, scanning the surrounding forest for potential dangers, Elianna stood next to me.

"You don't want to sleep, Starlight? I don't imagine we'll stay here for too long. You should rest while you can."

Elianna shrugged and wrapped her arm around my waist, nuzzling into my side. "I hate that you're stuck out here. I know you're just as tired."

Holding my mate against me, I leaned over to kiss her on the top of her head. "I am tired, but I need to keep watch, at least for now. The Oathornes should show up soon. I don't want to leave without them, but I don't think it's safe to stay here for long." I kissed her again, rubbing my hand up her back. "I'll be okay out here. Get some rest with Zoe."

Smiling up at me, Elianna stood on the tips of her toes to give me another kiss before walking away and climbing into the tent. I watched her as she retreated, a lovesick grin on my face. She didn't know what she did to me, how badly I'd wanted to claim her last night, how desperately I wanted to get her back to our home. It was on my mind as I watched the forest, trying to make out any movement in the chaos.

Baltair had picked out the campsite because it was far from the beaten path and surrounded by dense trees and brush, making us invisible to anyone passing by. The clearing where our tent stood, and our small fire burned, had been barely large enough for the four of us when we'd stayed there days earlier. Since there was so much natural protection, I didn't expect us to be found there, at least not by anyone aside from the Oathornes, but I wasn't willing to bet my mate's life on it if I abandoned my watch to sleep. So, I patrolled the small perimeter, sword in hand, until the sun set behind the tree canopy, and until the two human women awoke and exited the small tent to warm by the fire.

The sound of nearly silent footfalls caught my attention just as Elianna stepped toward me. Holding my hand up to her, I signaled for her to stop walking. I listened again, my gifted fae hearing straining against the sounds of insects and animals, but I heard it again. Someone was coming, and they were trying to remain unseen. With my body tensed, and using only rough hand signals, I motioned for the females to climb back into the tent. To my relief, they didn't argue and did as asked. If someone were to happen upon us, I needed to appear alone.

My heart pounded against my ribcage, my instinct to flee with my mate undeniable, but the steps were too close for me to chance running. I couldn't lose her, not after I'd just found her, but if we were caught... My fear was palpable as I scanned the darkness for the intruder.

The whistle came first, low and natural, and so like the sound of a bird that the untrained ear may have discounted it, but I knew better.

"It's just us, brother." The low voice was like a warm blanket on my nerves. I would recognize Fionn's voice anywhere. When the older Oathorne brother walked through the dense brush and into the clearing, I couldn't have been more relieved to see him.

A deep exhale rushed out of me as all three males came into view. "I cannot tell you how glad I am to see the three of you."

Baltair smiled, the older male patting me on the shoulder as he moved toward the fire. "I take it you found her?"

"I did." Walking toward the tent, I motioned for Zoe and Elianna to come back out. "And the medicine for your grandson?"

Fionn patted his cloak pocket as he unstrapped the sword from his belt. Dropping his pack on the ground, Cailean saluted me before pulling out their tents. Fionn helped his brother to set them up as their father brewed tea. True to their usual routine, the Oathorne males would undoubtedly want to rest during the day and travel at night. With them showing up at the campsite, I could rest as well, removing some of the burden from my shoulders.

Peeking her head through the tent flap, Elianna

smiled and stepped out. I pulled her into my arms, kissing her and then escorting her to the fire. I introduced her to Baltair, the older male, visibly delighted, before introducing my mate to Baltair's sons as well. There was an ease about Elianna, even in stressful situations, that made people want to get close to her, get to know her.

Zoe came out a short time later, Cailean showing undeniable interest in talking to her, even with their own mates' fate still unknown. As lonely as it could be for a male in Ecromos, I understood. They were the only two in the group who were unmated. I knew Zoe's mate would look for her, any male would, but I couldn't fault either of them if they ended up looking for companionship in each other, at least for a little while.

Cailean took the first watch, so I returned to my tent with Elianna while Zoe took the tent that the younger brother wasn't using. We wouldn't be able to sleep for long, but with us planning to set out as a group at nightfall, we needed to rest while we could. After all the time on the back of my horse with Zoe in tow, I was looking forward to being alone with Elianna, even if the others would be within hearing distance of our tent. I knew we couldn't do much other than sleep, but even just holding her would have been enough for me, at least for the moment.

"We're getting closer to our soft bed," Elianna said as she slipped her arm across my abdomen. Her touch and the implications of her statement sent a wave of heat through my body, warming me even on a chilly night. I wanted her so badly I could taste it. She was my mate, and, although she wanted me to claim her, I'd yet to do so. It was becoming more challenging to resist the siren call of her body through our mating bond.

Threading my fingers through her short, silky hair, I tipped her head back and kissed her. The touch of my tongue against hers was luxurious, a promise. "Hopefully." Another kiss, this time to her cheek. "The next time." I kissed her neck, Elianna leaning into the touch, her breath catching. "We stop to sleep." Returning my lips to hers, I ran my tongue along the seam of her mouth, dipping inside to taste her. "We'll have that soft bed."

She nodded, and I kissed her one more time before tucking her against me. "Maybe, since I have something so good to look forward to, it'll help me be braver while we travel through the forest tonight."

With my arms around her, I squeezed her in a warm embrace, taking in her intoxicating scent. "You're the bravest person I know, my Starlight."

CHAPTER TWENTY-FOUR

Elianna

With six people staying at our campsite, there was increased safety, but not necessarily more quiet. The males weren't trying to make noise; they just couldn't help it. Thankfully, even with so many of them around and no luxury bedding, I had slept through the afternoon, not even stirring when Blaze woke up to take his turn on watch.

I had met the Oathorne males before returning to the tent to sleep. I took to them immediately, especially the father, Baltair. He was kind and clearly someone who loved his family, which made my heart ache a little, as he reminded me of my own father. Even with my connection to Blaze and the closeness we had developed since he rescued me, I still missed my parents when things got quiet.

I had Blaze, but I couldn't forget about Zoe, who had become an important part of my life. My friend was adaptable and resilient, effortlessly charming the Oathorne males. Zoe's likability was just part of who she was. Hearing her whispers from outside, I pulled on my boots and exited the tent.

The smell of roasted meat lured me toward the fire, where Cailean was cooking a large rabbit over the flames. Blaze stood at the perimeter, sword in hand, whispering to the oldest Oathorne brother. Although Blaze told me that Fionn had a wife and children, there was a roughness about him I couldn't quite decipher. It was clear that he hadn't always been settled down with a family; he may have once been a warrior or even a mercenary. There was so much about the fae world that I didn't know, but I was eager to learn more.

Blaze turned and grinned at me as I approached the fire. The way he looked at me made my knees weak. He was the one thing in this new world that was truly mine, and I was his. It was strange, this instant attraction and deep need for someone I barely knew. The magic in our keys must have been strong—or whatever force it was that drew us together. Whatever the cause of my deep feelings for him, I wasn't afraid.

"How did you sleep?" Zoe's voice caught me by surprise; I had been so lost in my own thoughts.

Shrugging, I turned toward my friend and away from my mate. "As well as could be expected. I'm definitely ready to be somewhere safer, somewhere more permanent."

"Anything is better than the manor, but I am definitely looking forward to that, too. I just wish I knew if there was anyone on the other side of this connection." The golden key in Zoe's hand flickered once before going dark again. "What happens if he never shows up? Am I just supposed to wait for him?"

Honestly, I didn't know the answer to Zoe's question, but I had to say something. "I'm not sure who makes those decisions. But really, Zoe, it should be up to you whether you keep that key or toss it in the grass. You're the one who chooses how to spend your future and with whom. I support you either way, and I know Blaze would completely support you staying with us as long as you need to."

Zoe glanced at the metal object in her hand before sliding it back into her pocket. "I don't think I'll give up on him yet, whoever he is. Until he finds me, however, I'm just going to live."

After we finished eating the roasted meat and packed up the camp, we set out on our journey to the Court of Harmony. With more horses now in our party, Shadow no longer had to carry three people on her back, something I was sure she appreciated. I still rode with my mate, but Zoe climbed onto the horse with Cailean. Since they were the only two in the group without mates—at least none they had met—it made sense for them to share a horse.

As we traveled miles away from the main path through the forest, everything was quiet. The trek to Blaze's home would take several days and would be less than comfortable, but it was necessary. There were undoubtedly individuals looking for us, so we couldn't travel on the road or risk stopping at an inn. Blaze had told me about how they had been followed and attacked after their stay while on their way to find me, and no one wanted that to happen again. Therefore, at least until we arrived safely at Blaze's home court, we would have to do without a proper bath or a comfortable bed. However, I couldn't complain; I was in good company, and the inconveniences and discomforts were only temporary.

With one hand on Shadow's reins, Blaze used his other arm to hold me gently against his chest. Even in the dark forest, guided only by the sliver of moonlight and my companions' keen sense of sight, I felt safer than I had in a long time. I leaned back against him, the steady beating of his heart soothing my worries.

"Are you cold?" he asked. Unfastening the clasp of his cloak, Blaze wrapped it around me as well. I couldn't help but grin, even though he couldn't see it in the darkness. With the warm fabric of his cloak around my shoulders, his woodsy, masculine scent filled my senses, warming me both inside and out.

"I'm not anymore," I replied.

"Good." Keeping our voices low, Blaze spoke directly into my ear, his breath warming my cheek. "What are you looking forward to most when we're home?"

There were so many answers to that question, and I filtered through them, trying to decide on the best one to voice. "I guess what I'm looking forward to the most is just the day-to-day. Does that make sense?"

After all the years I'd spent being sick and not knowing how many tomorrows I had left, I looked forward to living in every moment. But I didn't know how to explain that to someone who had never had those worries. Blaze was quiet for a moment, but his arm around my waist tightened—a way of showing me he was there, not just physically, but in every way. "It makes sense. After being alone for so long, it's difficult to imagine how my life will change, but I look forward to every experience we'll share."

There were many experiences I was looking forward to having, including one in a soft bed. "And what about your home? Is it ready for a woman? No laundry lying around on the floor?"

Blaze chuckled, nuzzling into my neck to place a kiss against my skin. "I'd be lying if I said I didn't live like a bachelor, but I'm not a slob. If that's what you're asking."

"A bachelor, huh?" I poked him in the arm, joking

but only slightly. The thought of other women having been in his life made me feel a bit jealous.

This time, when he nuzzled into my neck, he playfully bit me. "Not a bachelor in that way. I vow that my bed is cold—icy, even. I've been waiting for you for a very long time."

It was at that moment that I realized I'd never even asked him how old he was. I knew that fae aged slowly, and Blaze looked no older than his mid-twenties, but that wasn't an accurate indicator of his age. We'd never discussed my age either. "How old are you, anyway?"

When he chuckled again, I realized the number was probably higher than I expected. I had so few experiences in my brief life—even fewer than most people my age. My mate, however, had likely lived lifetimes. "Let's just say I'm much younger than Baltair."

I poked him again, harder this time. "That's not an answer, and you know it."

Grabbing my finger, Blaze pulled it into his mouth and bit it just as he had bitten my neck. "I'm in my fifth decade, just like Cailean. And you?"

If I were honest, I'd expected the number to be higher, and I almost felt embarrassed to admit my age. If we were back in the human world, he would undoubtedly be considered a cradle-robber. Just thinking about it made me giggle on the inside, but I also cringed. "I'm afraid you're too old for me, sir.

I'm only nineteen."

"Is that so?" I didn't think his voice could go any lower, but it did, making my toes curl in my boots. The arm around my waist lowered until his hand slid up my thigh. "I guess I'll have to prove to you that I'm not too old to keep up with you, then."

There was a challenge in his words—one I was one hundred percent on board for. I forced some of my old swagger into my response, pulling forth the aloof attitude I had left behind when I had been dropped inside the portal on my last breath. "I guess you will."

Our whispered conversation slowed over the next several hours as Blaze focused on listening for any potential dangers in the forest. The trees thinned out for several miles, allowing the moonlight to illuminate our surroundings and ourselves. This made the need to remain silent even more crucial. Shadow led our group, with Cailean and Zoe following closely behind, Baltair nearby, and Fionn bringing up the rear.

Mist rose from the leaf-littered ground, its tendrils

swirling like spirits through the vines hanging from the trees. I watched the eerie yet magical landscape as we passed, the hoots of owls and howls of large animals sending chills down my spine. However, with Blaze holding onto me and the other three males in our group, I felt safe, even though I was uncertain about what strange creatures inhabited those woods. Occasionally, I'd startle myself, my eyes playing tricks on me in the shadowy darkness, but my mate seemed to sense my fear and held me tightly for reassurance.

When the sun finally rose over the horizon, barely visible under the dense tree cover, we found ourselves bathed in light once again. I felt relieved—not only did it mean I was no longer surrounded by obscurity, but it also signaled a chance for us to rest. Although I had merely been riding on Shadow's back throughout the night, it had still been exhausting and painful. My backside and thighs were sore and stiff, so I was more than ready to dismount when the males finally selected a small clearing near a stream to camp for the day.

Once we dismounted and set the horses in a safe place to graze and drink, the males began setting up camp while Zoe and I used the stream to clean up and refill our water skins. The small deer Cailean had killed just as the sun rose was being prepared to roast over the fire. I slid into the tent I shared with Blaze, while Zoe returned to the tent she had slept in at our last camp. Since Cailean was busy preparing the meat, Fionn offered to take the first watch, allowing Blaze and Baltair to rest for the first half of the day. Once the horses were tended to, Blaze went to clean up in the stream while I waited for him in our tent. Though we still lacked the privacy and soft bed we had hoped for at our next stop, it wouldn't stop me from holding and kissing my mate until we could enjoy more time together.

CHAPTER TWENTY-FIVE

Blaze

The night had been exhausting, and I could feel the fatigue settling in as I washed in the stream. If I had to guess, we were close to the border of the Court of Harmony—maybe half a day's ride from my cottage near its northern edge. We were so close I could almost taste it, but still too far to make it without stopping. If it had been just my mate and me on this journey, I would have probably pushed on or at least planned for a shorter stop. However, with the oldest of the Oathorne males needing longer breaks to rest, we had to adjust our pace.

Our group hadn't been alone in the forest, though I kept that to myself. I didn't want to alarm Elianna or the others unless the threat became more imminent. I heard footsteps in the distance—too faint to catch without my stronger hearing—but they hadn't come close enough for me to raise any alarms. There was no talking or the sound of many hooves. Whoever was nearby was only traveling with one or two horses. Since I only heard a few steps, I didn't think it could have been Lord Argall's guards, but it was still a possibility.

I chose not to tell the others about the distant footsteps trailing behind us. My conversation with Elianna had halted when I first heard those sounds; traveling with my mate, my entire body had tensed at the nearness of other travelers. I only began to relax a bit once we stopped to make camp, and that was primarily due to what I had learned about Baltair earlier that day.

While on watch with the oldest brother at our last campsite, Fionn explained that their father had the power to erect masking wards. I had always wondered why the Oathorne males seemed unbothered by making camps in the middle of the day—during times when they would be most visible—but now I realized that was because we weren't visible at all, at least not to most. Though the magic didn't work when we were on the move or when Baltair's energy was low, the patriarch could mask our camps most of the time, allowing us the safety to rest without the added threat of being seen. I hadn't known about this power when I first encountered them in the forest; that was because they had just made camp that day. Baltair had still been tapping into his power when I approached them, which contributed to his need for rest afterwards.

Elianna's eyelids were heavy, but she was still awake when I entered the tent. She grinned at me, the gesture genuine despite our exhausting travels and uncomfortable lodging. Given everything she had been through—freedom from captivity and disease—this small joy seemed to be enough for her.

I fully intended to provide her with so much more when we returned home: a life filled with love and safety.

"I was hoping you'd show up before I fell asleep," she said.

Kicking off my boots, I dropped down beside her, sliding my arm around her waist. "Looks to me like you're nearly there," I replied.

It was impossible not to admire her face—her bright blue eyes and delicate features. I gently tucked a lock of her chestnut hair behind her forehead, captivated by how soft her skin felt. The thought of her velvet skin against mine, with nothing between us, sent a rush of blood to my groin, making me feel stiff and throbbing. "You really are beautiful, my Starlight. Absolutely breathtaking."

Her eyes seemed to brighten at my words, as if she had never been told such things before, which was hard for me to believe. She was beautiful inside and out. Leaning closer, Elianna wrapped her arm around my neck and tangled her fingers in my long hair, pulling it free from its binding. "You're not so bad yourself, my love. You definitely have better hair."

The pull of the mating bond made it impossible for me to refrain from kissing her any longer. I wrapped my arms around my mate, pulling her against my chest as our lips touched in another promise. Tomorrow, I would claim her and make her mine in every way we both desired.

The sound of Cailean's frantic voice broke the silence as he called out Zoe's name. Jolting up from the spread of blankets, I quickly pulled on my boots and darted out of the tent, with Elianna following just a moment later.

As I stepped closer to the fire, I saw the youngest Oathorne brother disappear into the brush, Fionn chasing after him. I stood there for a moment, trying to comprehend what had happened. Cailean's frantic screams indicated that whatever had transpired was serious.

Midway between our tent and the fire, Elianna approached me, her eyes wide with worry. "What happened, Baltair? Where's my friend?"

The older male sitting near the fire cleared his throat before pointing toward the denser part of the forest. "They've gone after the blond female. Cailean went to check on her, but she wasn't in the tent. No one saw her leave the camp, but she's not here."

Elianna gasped and sprinted in the same direction the brothers had just gone, but I grabbed her hand, stopping her before she ran off. "I need you to stay here in the wards with Baltair, Starlight. I can't have you disappearing, too."

Without waiting for me to finish my plea, she shook her head. "No way, Blaze. She's my friend. I have to find her."

I scanned her face, dread burning in my chest at the thought of losing her. Anything could happen if she left the protective wards of the campsite and ventured into the forest. "Elianna... please. If you're with me, my focus will be on you. I won't be able to pay attention to finding your friend. If I know you're safe here, then I can concentrate solely on Zoe."

As I waited for her response, expecting her to stubbornly insist on following me into danger, I saw a realization wash over her. The change was evident in her eyes, her hands loosening in mine, her expression reflecting defeat. "She didn't run, Blaze. She wouldn't. Someone took her. Please find her."

I nodded, pulling Elianna into a warm embrace and kissing her hard before looking over my shoulder at Baltair. "Protect her with your life."

After one last kiss on my mate's lips, I reluctantly let her go and ran toward Shadow, hoisting myself into her saddle before charging off toward my two friends.

With my senses on high alert, I maneuvered my horse through the dense trees, searching for any sign of Zoe or the two males trying to find her. We hadn't been at the campsite long, so Zoe shouldn't have gotten far, whether she left on foot or was taken on someone else's horse. I held my sword at the ready, the hood of my dark cloak pulled up over my hair to help me blend into the shadows.

After a few miles of navigating through thick trees

and brush, I found all three of them, but I couldn't approach—not with the six males who had her bound and gagged. Elianna was right; Zoe hadn't run. She had been taken.

Dismounting Shadow, I couldn't fathom how the female had been captured by Baltair's guards as I moved silently toward where Fionn and Cailean were hiding behind a cluster of trees. I suspected she might have left their safety to relieve herself, not realizing the danger that lay ahead.

The female was limp in one of the guards' arms, likely due to someone's magical influence rather than physical harm, though I couldn't be sure. Regardless, she couldn't fight back or escape.

The group of guards under Lord Argall's command seemed overly confident in their ability to remain unnoticed as they set up a small camp. Either they believed they would go unobserved, or they didn't care if they were discovered. They had traveled just as far as we had, so they would need to stop and rest as well. They were likely either tired or unwilling to move on until they reclaimed both women.

From what Elianna had told me, she would have been auctioned off, with the lord expecting to earn a significant amount of coin from her sale due to her purity. The thought of it made my stomach churn. I appreciated that my mate had never been touched by another male. My possessive fae instincts craved her entirely for myself, but that did not enhance her worth to me, nor did it change my feelings for her.

Realizing the guards remained close by to recapture my mate, a large part of me wanted to climb back onto Shadow and return to our camp to protect her. However, I couldn't do that. Zoe was Elianna's friend, and she counted on me to rescue her. After all she had lost, I refused to add Zoe to the list of things my mate would have to grieve.

Being only a couple of hundred yards away from the lord's guards, my companions and I needed to stay quiet. Fionn signaled for us to split up. With six visible guards and only three of us, we were at a disadvantage. Our only option was to divide and conquer.

I nodded in agreement, and the Oathorne brothers vanished into the brush, Cailean moving to the left and Fionn to the right. I scanned the camp again. Six guards were visible, but with four tents, it was likely there were more asleep inside. Though Zoe hadn't been gone long, the chances were high that only a few guards had followed us while others remained to watch over their camp.

No longer held by the guard, Zoe lay unconscious

just inside one of their tents. I couldn't see her face, but I could make out the brown fabric of her trousers through the open tent flap from my position.

A fire blazed in the center of the camp, with one guard tending to the deer roasting over it while the others watched the perimeter. The male closest to my hiding spot stared straight at my location but didn't seem to see me. Given the chaotic spread of plant life surrounding me, I wasn't surprised. With my dark cloak and clothing, I was well camouflaged.

As I continued to survey the camp from my crouched position, I noticed the guard nearest Zoe's tent being pulled into the forest. Cailean had subdued him before he could offer any resistance.

The chatter of birds fell silent moments later, filling me with an uneasy sense of foreboding. I swallowed hard, trying to steady my breathing as I watched Cailean move closer to the tent where Zoe was being held.

Suddenly, I felt the cool metal of a blade against the crook of my neck. My attacker's footsteps had been so stealthy that I hadn't heard them approaching; I had been too distracted.

"Drop your sword, and maybe we'll let the female live," the guard hissed in a cruel drawl. "We were only ordered to return the short-haired one alive. It seems the blond doesn't matter to anyone but you."

CHAPTER TWENTY-SIX

Elianna

I had promised to stay at the camp and wait for Blaze, but the longer I waited for his return, the harder it became to keep my word. The mating bond held tight, reassuring me that he was still alive, but he wasn't close—nowhere near close enough for me to stop worrying. I paced around the fire, my boots tearing up the grass until only churned dirt remained.

"That's it. I'm going to look for them," I declared.

The male in charge of looking after me, Baltair, shook his head, running his fingers through what little hair he had left.

"It's not safe in the forest. We wouldn't want to be gone if Blaze, Zoe, or one of my sons comes back. The safest thing for us to do is follow Blaze's orders and stay put. Whatever Zoe's gotten herself into, the three of them can handle it."

Everything in me wanted to trust that Baltair was right, that my friends and my mate were safe and on their way back. But I couldn't shake the feeling that something was off—both with my bond to Blaze and Zoe's sudden disappearance, which had occurred just after we made camp. If Zoe had been re-captured by Lord Argall's guards, why hadn't I been taken as well? What had Zoe done to make herself a target when we were supposed to be in a warded space? Maybe Zoe had unknowingly stepped outside the boundary.

Turning on my heel, I began pacing in the opposite direction.

"If they've all been captured by Lord Argall, they could be halfway back to Cloudfell without us even knowing. We have to go after them. We can leave a note or carve something on a tree, but we must search for them. They might need our help."

I clenched my teeth as I waited for Baltair's response, expecting another argument. But he merely huffed out a breath and stood from the log he had been sitting on.

"Get yourself ready. Dress warmly and wear multiple layers under your cloak. If you need clothes, you can borrow some of mine or one of my sons. It doesn't matter if they don't fit; all that matters is that you're protected. I want every bit of your skin covered, so make sure the hood on your cloak is pulled low. Attach as many weapons to yourself as you can—swords, daggers, knives, or even a stick, for all I care. Just make sure you're armed. I'll do the same, and I'll meet you back by the fire in ten minutes."

That was the last thing he said before he stormed

away, climbing into the tent he shared with Fionn.

My heart pounding in my ears, I dashed into my own tent to follow his instructions. I had little in the way of extra clothes—only what Pith had given to me and Zoe—but I put on all the layers I had: a pair of trousers, long socks, boots, and a tunic. Then I rummaged through Blaze's pack and pulled out a jacket, gloves, and a long black cloak, fastening it around my neck and pulling the hood down to my eyebrows.

Blaze had most of our weapons, leaving only a couple of daggers and an extra sword, but I wasn't sure how best to attach them to my body. I had never needed weapons in my old life, but in this new world of danger and uncertainty, they were essential for survival. So, I took them back to the fire where Baltair could help me.

While I waited for him to come out of his tent, I walked to the stream and filled up three water skins, stuffing them into the pack slung over my shoulder before returning to the fire. By the time I got there, Baltair was already waiting, sitting on a log and lacing up his boots.

"I've never worn or used daggers or swords before, so if you could show me how to carry them without injuring myself, then I'll be ready to go," I said.

He looked up at me with an arched white eyebrow before smiling. "I'm not surprised you have no experience with weapons, but I trust Blaze will change that once he gets you back home. A male like him will want to ensure his female can protect herself at any moment when he's not with her. He'll be an excellent mate for you."

"Here," he said, holding out his hand. "Hand me that sword."

I obliged, not only handing Baltair the sword but also setting two daggers down in front of his boots. My cheeks warmed at his comments about Blaze. Having a mate was such a new concept to me, but it reassured me that others saw so much good in him.

Baltair wasted no time strapping the weapons onto me, explaining how to do it properly for my future use. I watched every step as if my life depended on it—because it did. If I ventured into the forest and needed to save my mate or my friends, I had to know how to access my weapons. I couldn't afford to think of failure. If I were unprepared and something happened to them, it would be my fault. So, I watched Baltair unblinkingly as he showed me how to attach my weapons to my body and how to remove them from their holders when needed. I vowed to myself to ask Blaze to teach me self-defense once our lives calmed down and we were in a safe place. He still didn't know about my powers, which probably played a big part in why he hadn't let me accompany him to find Zoe. But I would tell him as soon as I could. I needed to learn not only how to use my powers but also how to wield weapons when my powers failed.

We left the camp shortly thereafter. The mating bond, like a golden string connecting me to my mate, guided our way. Blaze had left on Shadow's back, which meant he could have gone much farther in a short time than we realized. Climbing onto Baltair's horse, Enchantress, we hoped to make up for lost time with the bond pulling me in the right direction. I knew little about our connection yet, but I had already noticed how my body reacted when he was nearby versus when he wasn't. Even if I couldn't see Blaze in the dense forest, the bond would tell me when he was close; the pull would become less pronounced and less insistent. It felt like a childhood game of hide-and-seek, except the person hiding held onto a roll of yarn, allowing it to unravel as they went.

After an hour of riding through the dense trees, the bond tugged me north. Baltair kept his eyes on his compass while we followed the pull of the invisible string without question.

We rode for a few miles; the chaotic sights and sounds of the forest made me wonder if we had traveled anywhere at all. Everything looked the same—until I heard the first sound of someone's voice, someone who was not from our group.

The horse's steps slowed as the voices grew closer, and the tug of the mating bond slackened—a sign that Blaze was nearby. We dismounted, allowing the horse to step away as Baltair and I crept closer, crouching behind a natural blind of bushes.

Four of Lord Argall's guards sat near a fire, gnawing on the bones of some roasted animal. After spending time in his manor, I recognized their solid black uniforms. Scanning the clearing, Baltair remained silent beside me. My blood ran cold. We were in so much trouble.

Blaze and Cailean stood on the far side of the fire, their bodies tied to tree trunks with ropes and their mouths gagged. My breath caught in my throat, and my heart raced as I searched the clearing again, looking for Zoe and Fionn. I had a strong feeling that my friend was being kept inside one of the tents, but I couldn't be sure.

"I don't see Fionn," I whispered to Baltair, keeping my voice as low as possible, although I realized Blaze might be able to hear me. His enhanced hearing was his superpower.

Concern furrowed Baltair's brow as he nodded. Before he could turn around, though, Fionn's enormous frame passed in our peripheral vision, approaching us from behind. I saw Baltair's shoulders visibly relax at the sight of his oldest son. Now, we just need to get the others back.

Gesturing for us to follow, Fionn led us deeper into the forest, with Baltair and me closely behind. Once we were far enough away to be out of earshot, Fionn turned to face us, looking visibly flustered.

"What happened?" I asked, my hands lifting at my sides before clenching into fists.

Fionn ran his fingers through his long hair, worry etched on his face. "We found where they were keeping Zoe rather quickly. The lord's guards had set up this camp, but we aren't sure how long they'll be here. Zoe was unconscious when we arrived, and we were outnumbered, so we split up to scout the camp from the perimeter. Cailean took out one guard, but Blaze was captured shortly after. I was across the camp when it happened. I saw the guard put the blade to his throat, but there was nothing I could do to stop it. Cailean tried to take down another guard, but one of his buddies was lying in wait and surprised him."

Baltair rubbed his palm down the side of his face, his eyebrows knitting together. "Is anyone hurt?"

Fionn shook his head. "I don't think so. Zoe's been unconscious, either under someone's power or drugged. They're keeping her in a tent. Blaze was brought in without incident. Cailean fought back, so he took a few hits, but they're probably nothing he hasn't already healed from."

I let out a breath as tears threatened to spill from my eyes. The only silver lining in this darkening forest was that my mate wasn't hurt. We just needed to rescue him before that changed. "So, what do we do now?"

"That's what I've been trying to figure out," Fionn replied, his jaw set and lips drawn into a thin line. "There are five guards we can see, but I don't know if any others are in the tents, and I'm unsure what powers they might have, if any. They're expecting something to happen. They plan to return to our camp to capture you." His dark eyes locked onto mine, dread coursing through me at the implications. "You're the reason they haven't left yet. The piece of work who captured Blaze told him that they weren't even here for Zoe. They're here for you."

That was the last thing I wanted to hear—that I was the reason my mate and two friends were in danger, possibly even losing their lives—but I wasn't surprised. The lord had made it clear how valuable I was to him, and he wouldn't let me go easily. My chest burned, and my limbs felt numb. Blaze didn't know about my powers, and I still didn't understand how to use them, but if those powers could help rescue my friends, I had to try.

Returning my gaze to my two companions—my only hope for rescuing our loved ones—I told them everything: how the healer had given me powers, what I had done to Lord Argall, and each little detail I knew.

When I finished speaking, Fionn raised an eyebrow,

a half-smile appearing on his lips. "I have a plan."

CHAPTER TWENTY-SEVEN

Blaze

I could have taken down the guard who had put a sword to my neck, but I didn't want to risk Zoe's life. I allowed the guard to drag me away and tie me to a tree, willing to sacrifice myself if the Oathorne males managed to get my mate out and rescue the other female, who was kept unconscious in a tent near the fire. With the other three males in my group being strong and resourceful, I wasn't too concerned about my capture. It was only a matter of time before they'd get me out. However, I could have done without Cailean getting captured as well. My confidence in being rescued was shaken a little by that setback.

Bound to a pine tree, the sap oozed into my clothes, making it difficult for me to move. If I ever got out of this predicament, I would have to burn every bit of fabric I was wearing. My attention was drawn to the right, where I watched Cailean throw his head back at the guard, breaking the male's nose and earning a boot to the back of his knee. The youngest Oathorne brother dropped to the ground before being pulled back up on shaky legs, with another guard joining the first to secure him to the tree nearest to me.

With the gags in our mouths, we couldn't speak, but I watched my friend, my eyes conveying what my voice couldn't: Don't fight. You'll only make it worse.

The guards had made two huge mistakes when securing me to the tree. They hadn't blindfolded me, nor had they plugged my ears. With my powerful hearing, I focused all my energy on listening to their conversations and Fionn's movements outside the camp. The male was discreet, but I could still tell exactly where he was by the cadence of his careful footsteps. What I hadn't expected to hear, what I hoped I had mistaken, was Elianna's voice.

My mate had only just entered my life, and she was already disregarding my advice, yet I couldn't help but grin against my gag. It seemed Elianna was just as stubborn as I was. I heard the voices of the two males accompanying her, and I listened as she told them about her newly discovered powers. A deep sense of pride bloomed in my chest. I still worried about her and hated that she was so close to danger, but it appeared I had underestimated her. If she had enough power in her tiny body to fling Lord Argall across the room and hold him there when he tried to touch her leg, she might have the strength to do the same to every one of his guards. Adding to my pride was how fiercely she had responded to the lord's unwanted advances, especially when she had been so open to my own affections. If I ever got out of this, I wouldn't waste any time claiming her in a soft bed.

By the time Elianna's brilliant blue eyes peeked at me through the bushes again, I knew they had a plan. I winked at her, hoping she realized I had heard their entire conversation and her secret. It wasn't unheard of for a healer to transfer some of their power to a human during the healing process, but it wasn't common either. The question was: Did the guards know about her powers? Would they expect her to use them?

Three more guards had emerged from tents after my capture, totaling eight, including the guard Cailean had killed before being detained. One guard stood watch over Zoe at the entrance of the tent where she was kept, while the others staked out the perimeter of the camp. I knew they intended to return to my camp to abduct Elianna, but unfortunately, they wouldn't find her there. That was one more reason for me to be glad she had ignored my warning.

Although I had expected Lord Argall to be with his men, he had yet to appear. The lord could have been hiding in one of the several tents in the clearing, but I was starting to believe that wasn't the case. It wasn't surprising; why would a wealthy male like Lord Argall venture on a multi-day journey through the wilderness, getting his hands dirty, when he had others to do it for him? The spoiled bastard was probably lounging in his apartments, enjoying a fine meal and abusing his servants while others did his dirty work. I couldn't suppress my loathing for the lord, especially after hearing how he had tried to touch my mate. If I ever got the chance, he wouldn't be the one walking away unscathed.

A sharp whistle echoed across the clearing, easily mistaken for a bird's call by an unsuspecting listener, but I recognized it as Fionn's signal. I watched as recognition sparked in Cailean's eyes—the youngest Oathorne perked up at the sound. Thankfully, none of the guards seemed to notice; a few continued their conversations as they patrolled the camp's perimeter.

I tugged at the knot behind my back, the sap between the strips of rope making them slippery.

Another whistle sounded, drawing the guards' attention. A few exchanged glances and communicated through hand signals before two of them walked off into the forest. Fionn was undoubtedly waiting for this moment. Cailean, noticing my efforts to loosen my restraints, began working on his own. With the guards distracted by the potential risks to their perimeter, they were no longer concerned about their two captives, confident that our bindings would hold. However, I was more confident in my ability to escape.

Elianna had stopped peering through the brush. When they made their plans, Baltair insisted she stay hidden. She had argued, insisting on saving us, which only made me love her more. But the Oathorne patriarch didn't want to take any risks.

As honorable as her desire to save us was, and despite her strengths, she was still too inexperienced to confront trained fae guards. Baltair understood that, and so did I. I could only hope my brave mate came to the same conclusion.

The guards who had ventured into the forest hadn't returned, and soon after, another guard was sent after them. I listened as his footsteps faded into the distance, and I knew when they ceased. I didn't need to see into the trees to understand that Fionn was out there, taking them down one by one.

As soon as another guard was out of sight, I intensified my efforts to break free from my restraints, with Cailean doing the same beside me. I pressed my arms against the tree, the bark cutting into my flesh as it wore against the fibers of the rope. Sap and blood mixed, creating a slippery barrier. While the sap's healing properties would aid my wounds eventually, for now, I winced as I increased the friction. Moments later, I felt my bindings snap—the fibers of the rope hot from the intense contact with the rough bark of the tree.

I stood still, scanning the clearing to ensure the guards hadn't noticed my escape before moving to help my friend. Four guards were stationed at the perimeter, chatting among themselves and glancing toward the spot where their comrades had disappeared. One of them was the guard who had been watching over Zoe; he had abandoned his post to help monitor the camp's edges. This was the perfect opportunity to rescue her, provided we could act quickly while the guards were distracted.

Fionn, likely watching from an unseen location, seemed to anticipate my needs. Another sharp whistle pierced the silence, causing all four guards to dart toward the forest in pursuit of the source of the noise. Four guards at once were a lot for Fionn to handle alone, so I hoped that Baltair was out there to assist him instead of Elianna. But I couldn't focus on that right now; I had to free Cailean so we could get Zoe out of the camp before the guards returned.

Pulling off my gag and tossing my sap-covered, bloody rope and cloak to the ground, I sprinted toward the tree where Cailean was bound. He was still trying to free himself. Ignoring the pain in my torn hands, I worked to loosen the knots on Cailean's restraints.

"When I set you free, Cailean, get Zoe and take her away from here. As far as you can. Go to my court, to my lands. We'll find you."

Once his hands were free and the ropes dropped to his feet, Cailean wrapped me in a tight embrace, gratitude spilling from his lips, before he dashed toward Zoe's tent. I ran in the opposite direction, drawn by the mating bond that pulled me forward. It didn't take long to find her, my steps faltering when she came into view.

"Stay back, and I won't slit her throat." The guard's words hit me like acid-laced arrows, targeted right at my heart, as he held a dagger to Elianna's neck.

Tears streamed down my mate's delicate cheek, tearing a hole in my heart. The urge to hold her and make her happy again clashed with the need to heed the guard's threats to ensure her safety. I raised my hands in surrender, not daring to step closer. "You don't want to harm her. Just let her go."

The guard's face twisted into something sinister. "With all my comrades gone, there's no one left to report back to Lord Argall about her. For all he knows, she and I both died, just like the rest of the guards." Spitting on the ground, he sneered, tightening his grip on Elianna's arm. She winced at his hold, tears falling, but she didn't fight back—not yet. "I don't have a mate, but I think this one would do just fine. After everything I've heard about her, I'd like a taste."

Rage ignited in my chest, spreading through my stomach and head. My hands turned into fists, my restraint wavering. I was ready to tear the guard apart for speaking about my mate in such a vile way. "Hopefully, you didn't taint her yet."

My fury reached a boiling point as I fixed my gaze on the dagger at Elianna's throat, willing it away with every fiber of my being.

Something in Elianna's expression shifted at the guard's words, revealing a woman ready for battle, one who was prepared to kill. When her eyes flicked up to meet mine, she grinned, sending a chill through me.

In an instant, the dagger pressed against her throat vanished. Instead, inexplicably, the guard was flung against a tree ten feet away, the dagger embedded in his chest.

CHAPTER TWENTY-EIGHT

Elianna

The moment I was grabbed from my hiding place by the guard who had slipped past Fionn and Baltair's trap, I had no intention of being taken alive. I would rather have died than been returned to Cloudfell to be sold, or worse, forced into the brothel.

When he grabbed my arm and pulled me against his chest, his dagger pressing against my neck, I felt the first surge of power inside me since Lord Argall had tried to touch my thigh. My muscles tensed, the pressure making my head swim. While some might have dismissed it as a rush of cortisol, my fight-or-flight instinct kicking in, I knew better. I didn't know how to control the power Hiedra had given me, but I recognized that it was magic I was feeling, not just a normal human response.

Fionn and Baltair were nowhere in sight, but that didn't mean they weren't close by. I had watched the guards as my friends lured them into the forest, taking them down one by one. The father-and-son duo had killed all of them, except for the male who held a knife to my throat. He had somehow gotten past them and found me.

The guard escorted me back toward the camp, and I walked in step with him, my eyes darting from side to side, searching for Fionn, Baltair, or anyone who could help me. When the guard yanked me into the clearing, I was not prepared to see my mate standing in front of us, blocking our path.

I could have sworn my heart stopped momentarily when Blaze darted forward, his momentum halting immediately upon seeing me and the dagger pressed against my flesh.

When the guard commanded Blaze to stay back or risk my life, the fear and desperation on his handsome face twisted into something I had never seen before. I struggled to hold back my tears, but it was a futile effort. I had tried to be strong, to show no weakness, but I couldn't help it, especially after witnessing the look on my mate's face.

Blaze was no longer wearing his cloak, and when he held up his hands in surrender, willing to do anything to keep me safe, I cringed at how bloody they were. He had clearly injured himself while trying to free himself, while also trying to save my friend. I thought of Zoe and Cailean. I wished I could ask Blaze if they'd at least gotten away, but I couldn't—not with the guard standing over me, not with his blade threatening my life if I moved.

My captor began to speak again, his words sounding like the ramblings of a madman—someone overwhelmed and without a real plan. I watched as Blaze's demeanor shifted with every word; his willingness to surrender faltered when the guard threatened to keep me for himself, to "taste" me.

The guard's words filled my stomach with dread, bile rising in my throat, threatening to spill over onto my boots. I saw the rage color Blaze's face, his knuckles whitening as he clenched his fists. His heightened emotions resonated with mine, sending a surge of energy through me. When the power threatened to escape from my body, my senses honed in on the guard's hands gripping my skin, his chest pressing against my back, and the blade resting against my throat. I let the power swell inside me, letting it spread through my limbs until it became unbearable; the pressure demanded an outlet, and I grinned.

Blaze stiffened, not realizing what was about to happen, because even I didn't know what my magic would do if I forced it out into the world. When I had used it against Lord Argall, it had been unintentional—a moment of intense stress where my instincts took over. That time, I hadn't had to think about it. It had just happened. This time, however...

The pressure in my body expanded until it had nowhere to go, the pounding in my head growing louder. My body tensed, and my skin felt electrified. I blinked, a breath escaping me, and the hands that had held me released their grip; the cool metal against my throat was no longer there.

When I opened my eyes, all I saw was Blaze. My mate rushed toward me, pulling me into his arms. The pressure inside me vanished, replaced by the weightlessness of release.

He kissed me deeply, claiming me, before pulling away to scan my face. "You're amazing, my Starlight. How did you do that?"

For a moment, I didn't understand his question. I didn't know what I had done. It wasn't until he looked over his shoulder, and my eyes followed his, that I saw the guard. Just like after Lord Argall had tried to touch my thigh, the male was now held helplessly against the tree trunk, thrown back by my power. Unlike the lord, however, this guard was dead.

Blood stained the black of his uniform where the dagger protruded from his chest. His eyes were unfocused and unseeing as he stared blankly into the distance. I gasped, the horror of what I'd done hitting me like a bolt of lightning. I knew I had acted in self-defense—he intended to take me and keep me for himself. He was going to...

As bile surged into my throat, I vomited, retching until there was nothing left. Blaze rubbed a gentle hand down my back, murmuring soothing words as I heaved. For a moment, the world spun around me.

Loud footsteps sounded behind us, but I barely reacted, too overwhelmed by my emotions and drained from the release of my untrained power.

"Are you two okay?" Fionn asked, holding a strip of fabric against a gash on his arm. Baltair, red-faced and sweating, stumbled into view.

I wiped my sleeve across my mouth and straightened onto shaky legs. Blaze wrapped his arm around my shoulders for support. "Thanks to my amazing mate, we're going to be fine."

Running his fingers through his tangled hair, Fionn let out a deep breath. "Have you seen Cailean or Zoe? There's no one left at the camp."

Blaze nodded, a grin spreading across his face as he looked down at me. "If at least one person followed my instructions today, they're on their way to the Court of Harmony. If we leave now, we can probably catch up with them along the way."

I cringed at his words. I had absolutely ignored Blaze when he pleaded with me to stay at our camp with Baltair. I didn't want to dwell on how the day's events might have unfolded if I had listened. Maybe next time, he'd allow me to join him if someone needed rescuing—although I hoped there would never be a next time. I had endured enough danger for one lifetime.

With the bodies of Lord Argall's guards respectfully buried, my mate, our two companions, and I set off on horseback toward the Court of Harmony. If we had had more time, we would have dismantled the guards' campsite, but we couldn't linger if we wanted to catch up with our friends. Since Zoe and Cailean's black mare was missing, we assumed they had gotten away.

Uncertain of our safety, we traveled in silence. With Lord Argall still unaccounted for, he could still be somewhere in the Whispering Forest with his guards. He might have returned to his estate after failing to find the runaway women in Cloudfell, but we couldn't know for sure. It was more important than ever for Blaze to remain vigilant for any potential risks.

We traveled for hours, and by the time we left the cover of the forest and stepped onto the plains in the Court of Harmony, the sun was nearly set. As the trees faded into the distance, so did my fear of recapture. There would always be risks; there was always a chance that the lord would come for me. However, entering the court of another king to steal a female would be an act of war. Blaze had mentioned this during our few conversations along the way, confident that no one could hear us.

I took a deep breath, the scent of the lavender fields in the distance calming me in a way I hadn't felt in years. "It's beautiful here."

Even with the sun setting, painting the sky in pastels of pink, purple, and orange, the land was wide open, filled with pastures and farms, flowers, and fields. It was nothing like the Court of Knowledge. Cloudfell was beautiful and bustling, but it lacked tranquility. It wasn't where I envisioned settling down and building a life.

Blaze kissed my cheek, his powerful arm pulling me closer. "Wait until you see my cottage. If you like this view, you'll love the view from the windows of our bedchamber. There are farmlands as far as you can see."

I liked the sound of that. A simple life was something I'd never experienced, but I knew I needed it. "I look forward to that." Breathing deeply, I leaned my head back to take in his face. We both needed a bath and clean clothes. The scruff on his face had grown longer, making him appear more rugged than when we first met. I liked it. "I look forward to a lot of things."

When Blaze's golden eyes looked down at me, the dark green outline more prominent against the darkening sky, I knew he understood. The half-grin on his face was wicked as he leaned down to kiss me, his hand moving to grip my inner thigh. For a moment, everything around us faded away, and all that mattered was his lips against mine, but Shadow's steps slowed, pulling us back to reality.

As we traversed the first several miles into my mate's home court, we hadn't caught up with Cailean and Zoe, but there were signs they had been there. Cailean, like Blaze, had the ritual of marking his path, leaving subtle clues only his father and brother would recognize. When we arrived at the first tavern along the well-traveled road leading into the capital city of Honeyhaven, I wasn't surprised to see the familiar mare secured in the stable next to it.

As we approached the wooden structure behind Baltair and Fionn, Blaze dismounted from Shadow and helped me down. A stable hand, a yellow-haired fae male no older than a teenager, called out to him by name. I realized that my mate had been here before.

I giggled at the sign in front of the building. The Clumsy Weasel Tavern had quite an interesting name, and the carving of a tiny animal downing a mug of ale next to the tavern's name was a perfect choice. Blaze seemed to notice my amusement and chuckled as he took my hand, leading me to the entrance.

The tavern was packed, but I spotted my friend right away. When Zoe noticed my approach, she rose from her stool and then collapsed onto the floor, burying her face in her hands. I dropped to my knees beside her, wrapping my arms around her trembling shoulders.

"When I was taken, I thought I'd never see you again," Zoe said, her voice shaking as she lifted her tear-stained face from her hands.

The guys stood back, with Cailean joining the others by the bar while Blaze spoke to the bartender. Holding Zoe's gaze, I wiped her damp cheek with my thumb. "But I'm here. We both are, and we're going to be okay."

Zoe nodded, but the tears continued to fall as she glanced at the bar patrons, all of whom had stopped their conversations to watch our reunion. She exhaled deeply and stood up, our hands interlocked. "So, we're free?"

Even though I wasn't sure that the risks were gone entirely, I couldn't burden her with that worry after everything we'd been through. We would still need to be cautious, at least for a while, but I kept that to myself as I smiled and squeezed Zoe's hand. "We're free."

CHAPTER TWENTY-NINE

Blaze

After everything we had gone through in the past few days, traveling four more hours to my cottage was not an option. With our arrival in the Court of Harmony, I knew we were safe—at least secure enough to spend the night in the inn atop the Clumsy Weasel Tavern. The barkeep was a friend, a man I had known since before our days in the war, when we fought against a common enemy. If anyone came looking for the two human females, Edric would send them on their way. Not that I was too concerned about it. Entering a foreign court and stealing someone would be an act of war, and no matter how high Lord Argall's rank, it wouldn't be an act he would commit without the support of his king. Not if he wanted to keep his head.

Feeling confident about our safety, I rented five rooms. According to Edric, the room I would share with my mate had the most comfortable bed. I grinned at the thought as I took the room keys from the bar and walked across the tavern, where the rest of my group was already sitting at a large table. Elianna was still holding Zoe's hand and beaming up at me when I sat in the chair next to her. Even after all she had suffered and everything she had given up, she remained a shining star.

When the server dropped off bowls of deer stew and mugs of ale at the table, we wasted no time digging in. We hadn't stopped to rest or eat since leaving the scene of our confrontation with the lord's guards, and everyone needed both.

Zoe still held her key, the metal object pulsing with light periodically. I noticed how Cailean looked at her; we all did. The younger male's own key had probably been silent. There were no guarantees with the way magic chose our mates, especially when choice played such an equal role. If his human mate had never crossed the portal into our world, he would never have received another key and would have lost his chance at what he wanted so badly. I couldn't blame the youngest Oathorne brother if he pursued Zoe. I didn't know how I would have handled it if Elianna had not made the choice she had—and if I had been left in the same position. Cailean was a good man, and he deserved love.

Baltair left to go upstairs to his room before the others. I was surprised the older male had stayed in the tavern as long as he did. When Fionn left the table to go to the bar, mumbling something about sending a letter to his mate, I used that as an excuse to take Elianna upstairs. As I left the tavern with my mate on my arm, the unmated pair was still at the table. Just as Elianna and I turned the corner to the stairwell, Cailean signaled the server for another pint of ale.

Elianna's eyelids were heavy as we climbed the stairs, her steps slowing once we reached the top, so I lifted her into my arms. She didn't argue; she only grinned at me and tucked her head into my chest. When I opened the door to our room, she breathed a sigh of relief. It wasn't home, but at least it wasn't a tent.

Even for the room that supposedly had the most comfortable bed, according to Edric, it was pretty small. For our purposes, however, it would do. The four-poster bed occupied half of the space, and a small wooden table stood against one wall, with the door to a bathing room situated on the other. Two windows allowed in a sliver of moonlight, but candles placed throughout the space lit it. I set Elianna down inside the room, pulling her against my chest and kissing her lips. She opened for me, and the kiss was deep but slow—a promise of what was to come.

"Bath?" I asked, motioning to the bathing room. Considering the room's size, the bathtub was quite large.

"Please." Her sleepy grin when she looked at the bathtub was enough to bring me to my knees. She trudged into the room, kicking off her boots before peeling off her cloak and dropping it to the floor.

Walking past her, I turned on the tap; the hot water ran after only a few moments. My eyes followed her movements as she reached for the laces on her trousers. When she caught me staring, her cheeks turned a brilliant shade of pink.

"Need some help?" I asked. As she fumbled with the laces at her waist, I reached for her hand, and she let me move it aside so I could take over.

I had always imagined that moment differently—our first time together—but I would have treasured any moment we had where we were safe.

"You're tired," I said as her trousers fell to the floor. Her blue eyes never left mine as I reached to untie her tunic next.

She reached for me, my hands pausing on her laces as she pulled my tunic over my head. "Not too tired."

I watched her for a moment before resuming my work on her laces, finding it difficult to look away from her beautiful face.

When the laces came free under my ministrations, Elianna's tunic slipped down one shoulder, and then the other, before dropping to the floor. Then she was there, naked in front of me, and she was perfect. I'd never expected my human female to be so petite when I was so large, but my size allowed me to protect her all the better, to take care of her, to *please* her. As I took in her breasts, the peaks already taut, my mouth went dry. My hand slid down the curve of her tiny waist, where it flared out at her hips, cupping her backside and pulling her against me. I wanted her to feel what being with her did to me. My cock was stiff against the inside of my trousers, throbbing, begging to be closer to her.

Steam filled the bathing room, the soaking tub nearly full. She didn't speak as my eyes traced her body, committing every curve, every freckle, to memory. When I led her into the tub, and she groaned as she slid into the hot water, it took every-thing in me not to claim her right there. We both needed it, but I wanted her to enjoy her bath, to experience the relaxation the warm water could give her, before I lay her down on the bed and worshiped her body until we were both spent.

Pulling a stool next to the head of the tub, I sat down, using a mug to pour water over her hair and shoulders, watching as it slid over her body, curl-ing around her nipples and down her flat stomach, before the droplets reunited with the water below. She closed her eyes as I bathed her, the sounds of pleasure coming out of her making my blood pump harder. When I lifted the mug to pour the water over her hair again, she grabbed my hand, pulled it towards her mouth, and kissed it. I shivered, think-ing of all the other things I wanted to put against her mouth.

"Come in with me?" Her voice was a low purr, and I felt the reverberations of it deep down.

"Do you want me to?" I already knew the answer, but I wanted her to hear it again.

Instead of speaking, she pulled my arm until I was

halfway in the tub and lying on top of her. I chuck-led as I went in headfirst, but just before my waist went below the surface, I stood back up to remove my trousers. If she was going to be naked, then I wanted to be too, wanting my skin against hers.

As I untied the laces around my waist, I realized she had never seen me entirely in the nude. She'd never been with *any* man. Not knowing what her reaction would be, I was filled with nerves about revealing myself to her. We'd rubbed against each other before. She'd even climaxed while straddling me and grinding against my length, but it wasn't the same as what we intended to do when she got out of the tub. I wanted her to like what she saw when I removed my trousers and didn't want to intimidate her with my size.

I knew I was a large male, especially compared to human men, and my mate was petite. She was inexperienced. Until that moment, I hadn't dwelled on whether I would hurt her or please her, but at that moment, when it was going to happen between us, it was on my mind. Still, the heavy-lidded look she gave me as I removed the last of my clothing told me she wasn't intimidated. She wanted me. Her eyes were wide as she took me in, her gaze tracing every curve of me, every detail, just as I had done with her. When her eyes traveled lower and her lip tucked between her teeth, I couldn't help but grin.

"See something you like, Elianna?"

My mate was so sexy as she lounged in the bath,

water dripping down her beautiful body, her lips plump from our kisses, and from her nibbling. Taking her hand, I let her pull me into the tub with her. I slid in behind her, wrapping my arms around her chest and sliding her back against me. There was no way for me to hide the hardened length that was against her back, but she didn't seem to mind. Instead, she twisted around, slipping her hands between us and gripping me, stroking her tiny hands up and down my shaft.

At the first touch of her skin against my cock, I closed my eyes and groaned, my hips bucking below the surface of the water. Her petite body fitting perfectly between my legs, she kissed me while pumping my length below the water. It took me by surprise, but I leaned back, threading my fingers into her short hair and deepening the kiss. The combination of the hardness of her grip and the softness of her mouth was exquisite, and I knew that if I didn't stop her, I was going to explode. I could already feel it building inside me, but I couldn't get my pleasure before she got hers. So, although my body objected, I removed her hand from where it held my cock and pulled her on top of me, her thighs straddling my abdomen.

"Not yet," I said, my voice a gentle caress. "When I finally get my release, I want it to be after you've had your first."

To my relief, Elianna didn't argue. She seemed to want to touch me as badly as I wanted to touch her. Sliding up my chest, she grabbed my hair, holding it in her hand as she pulled my face to hers. "As long as I get the chance to put my mouth on you, we can do it in whatever order you want."

I nearly climaxed right there at her proposition. She may have been inexperienced, but she was certainly ready for me and everything that being mates meant. "Then we should get out of this tub, because I don't know how much longer I can wait to taste you on my tongue and to sink inside of you until you're writhing beneath me."

Kissing me one more time, and licking across the seam of my lips, she stood, the water making rivulets down her body, drawing my attention to the apex of her thighs as she reached for a towel and dried off. With her standing right in front of me, it took all my strength not to lean forward and lick through her folds, to grab her hips and pull her against my face, to taste her. I'd wanted to do it since the first moment I'd seen her, and I couldn't wait much longer. At that moment, there'd been nothing else I'd wanted so badly. So, when she climbed out of the tub, I wasted no time going after her.

CHAPTER THIRTY

Elianna

When Blaze first brought me into the bedchamber, I'd been so tired, but with the sensual bath, and after seeing my mate's naked body for the first time, sleep was the last thing on my mind. I'd gripped his cock. Stroked it. It was something I'd never done before to anyone, but I was glad my first time had been with him. My first everything would be with him.

He'd been so patient with me and let me explore his body before he ever tried to touch me in those sensitive places. I wanted him to touch me, to take me, but he'd been a gentleman, waiting for me to ask for what I wanted. After all the rights that had been taken away from the women in Lord Argall's control, I appreciated his thoughtfulness and his respect. He'd stopped me, even when he'd been groaning with lust, lifting his hips to increase the friction of my hand around him. He'd still stopped me, because he wanted me to get pleasure first. With that offer, I dried off and climbed out of the tub without a thought. I was ready. If he wanted to get me into bed before touching me, then that was where I was going to go.

Having no clean clothes to speak of, and knowing

what was in store for the night, I climbed into the bed naked. Blaze entered the bedchamber a moment after I'd climbed onto the bed. A towel hung low on his hips as he dried his hair, the view sexier than he'd probably realized. I watched him while he watched me, neither of us taking the first step as I lay below the covers. Grinning at him, I pulled the blanket aside, exposing my body beneath.

"Are you going to come lie with me?"

It was the only invitation Blaze needed before he dropped the towel in his hands, and the one at his waist, and climbed into bed next to me. Sliding in beside me and wrapping his arms around me, Blaze pulled me against his chest.

"I expect nothing, Elianna." He kissed me, a featherlight touch on my lips. "If all you want to do is hold each other tonight, I would still be the happiest male in four courts. Don't think you have to do anything you aren't ready for, not for me."

His words were genuine, but I had no intention of just cuddling, no matter how long the day had been, no matter how tired we were. I needed him. Tangling my fingers into his hair, I tilted his head up, bringing his lips to mine. When I bit his lower lip just enough to hurt, he grinned against my mouth before opening for me, exploring me with his tongue. His knee slid between my thighs, and I ground myself against it. I moaned, the friction sending my eyes back into my head. Gripping my hips, he pulled me down against his leg, sending pleasure through my body as I undulated against it.

Our kisses became frantic, no longer staying on the lips. He trailed them down my neck, my breast, taking its stiff peak into his mouth and sucking. The sensation of it shot between my thighs, where I throbbed to be touched. He caressed my skin as his mouth worked, rubbing his hands across my stomach, my waist, circling my nipples before feeding the other into the warmth of his mouth. I squirmed on the bed below him, my hands itching to touch him, my mouth swollen to kiss him.

"Can I taste you?" Blaze's voice was nothing more than a rumble of sound, and my responding yes was barely a breath, but it was all he needed before lowering himself between my thighs and sliding one leg over his shoulder.

The first swipe of his tongue against my folds nearly sent me over the edge, my body arching off the bed, but he placed a calloused hand on my belly to hold me in place. He devoured me. I'd never felt anything so divine, so delicious, as his soft tongue worked against the most sensitive parts of me, the bundle of nerves sparking to life and building my climax with every swipe.

Gripping the blankets and pulling a handful into my mouth, I bit down on the fabric to stop the moans that threatened to wake the entire building. Blaze's groans, however, were not silenced. The sounds that came from him, from how much he was enjoying himself, brought me closer to the edge. A coil low in my belly tightened, making the emptiness between my thighs more desperate to be filled. I writhed against his mouth, needing more friction, needing him inside me. The moan that spilled from my mouth when he slid his finger inside me had probably been heard down the hall, but I didn't care. When he slid in a second one, I knew it had.

He worked my body, pumping his fingers inside me as he licked and sucked my clit, my movements becoming more frantic as I headed toward release. The coil low in my belly tightened, and tightened, and when it could tighten no more, it snapped. Release hit me like a tidal wave. I screamed, the aftershocks of it wringing out every drop of pleasure until I was boneless beneath him, but it wasn't the end. He'd given me pleasure, but I wouldn't take and not give, not like I had before. As soon as he pulled his fingers from inside me and kissed the inside of my thigh, I gripped him by his shoulders and tugged.

He crawled over me, a predator stalking its prey, and kissed me, the taste of me on his mouth filling me with steaming desire. "I want you," I breathed. "All of you."

Worry flashed across his face, and I kissed him again, but he pulled away to look into my eyes. "I'm not on a tonic... for pregnancy. With the numbers what they are... It's hard to get."

I placed my fingers against his lips, silencing him. "I knew that was a possibility when I came through the portal, when I looked for my mate, and I'm still here. If it happens between us now or later, I'll be happy. It doesn't change my mind about what I want from you or what I want to give to you."

Nodding, he kissed me again, settling his hips between my thighs. "So yes, then?"

"Yes."

Slipping his hand between our bodies, Blaze slid his length through my folds, my wetness coating his skin, before making the first nudge at my entrance.

I clenched my teeth, the first inch bringing with it a sting of pain, a feeling of being too full. Sensing my reaction, his body stiffened, his elbows that braced him on the bed restraining his movement. He leaned down to kiss me, slow and tender.

"Try to relax, my Starlight. I'll go slow. I don't want to hurt you. I don't want to do anything that you don't like. If it hurts at first, I'll go even slower, but I promise it won't hurt for long. And if you want to stop, we'll stop."

I nodded, blowing out a breath and forcing the

tension from my body.

He held his position while I adjusted to his size, the stinging fullness turning into a throbbing need after a few moments. I lifted my hips, encouraging him to move, to go deeper. Kissing me deeply, he did, slowly at first, slight movements to let me adjust. The more he gave, the more I wanted. I wanted him undone, wanted everything. Wrapping my legs around his waist, I pulled him forward, his barely contained restraint shattering as he surged into me, his thrusts becoming harder, deeper, until there was no space between us, until our bodies became one.

The passion I felt while Blaze's powerful body was on top of me, inside me, was more than I ever imagined sex could be. Our attraction was so powerful, so potent, that I thought we would burst into flames. My climax built again, the mind-blowing release coming in waves as he surged inside of me, the sounds he breathed in my ear only making the crests hit me harder.

When our movements became erratic, my release building again, he went over the edge with me, riding the waves together until we were only a panting heap of ecstasy and limbs.

Blaze claimed me as his mate, in mind, heart, and now body, and it had been the best moment of my life. I'd never experienced something so earth-shattering, and I felt so fortunate to have been chosen to be with him. I knew thoughts of my past life and my family would come back, needing to be processed, and I knew we'd have to go back to rescue the other women in Cloudfell, but at that moment, all that mattered was *us*.

Sliding off the bed, Blaze reached for the towel he'd discarded near the bed and returned to my side to clean me off. All I could do was watch him, his sated face set with concentration as he made sure I was comfortable. When he lay back down next to me, he pulled me against him, kissing me on the cheek.

"Are you okay?" His question was hesitant. I knew he worried that he'd hurt me, or that I regretted what we'd done, but neither was the truth.

Turning to face him, I cupped his cheeks in my hands and smiled. "I'm better than I've been in a long time."

Seeing his own smile, a genuine one that met his eyes, sent my heart aflutter. He rubbed his thumb down my cheek. "You really are perfect, Elianna. I don't know what I ever did to deserve you."

He meant everything he'd said, and I felt it deep inside my bones. "I feel the same way, but I'm sure you'll eventually find something about me that drives you crazy."

Chuckling, Blaze pulled me against him again, squeezing me tight. "I will even love your perfect flaws, my Starlight."

Even with the heartfelt conversation luring me to stay awake with him, exhaustion from the past few days, and the relaxation that followed such satisfying lovemaking, made my eyelids heavy. I yawned, tucking my head against his chest.

"Goodnight, Elianna." His hand made soothing strokes up and down my back as my eyes fell closed.

"Goodnight, my love."

CHAPTER THIRTY-ONE

Blaze

When I woke the next morning, it was with my mate warm in my arms, the sweet taste of her still lingering on my lips. Even in the tiny room of the inn, our night together had been magical. With her body against mine and the memory of being inside her, I couldn't get those moments out of my mind as I watched her sleep, listening to the soft sounds she made while dreaming. I found myself eager to make love to her again. Now that I knew what it was like to be with her, I realized I would never get enough. There was no one else who could ever compare to her. Elianna was everything to me. I could have stayed in bed all day. Edric was right when he said it was comfortable, but I needed to get my mate home. The Oathorne family needed a place where they could rest for a few days before continuing on to the rest of their family. I didn't know what that meant for Zoe or for returning to save the other females in Lord Argall's manor, either. My intention had been to save them all, but putting Elianna in danger again was out of the question. We would need enough warriors to ensure her safety if I decided to go back there.

As my mate lay comfortably next to me, her soft

skin warming my own, I couldn't bear to wake her. However, she awoke on her own as the sounds of people moving about the building penetrated the thin walls. This was yet another reason we needed to get home. Home offered safety, but it also offered privacy. As a newly mated male, I had to provide her with both.

When her blue eyes opened to meet my gaze, her expression was one of pure relief, happiness, and love. There were no longer dark circles under her eyes, no more fear. She smiled and snuggled closer to me as I held her.

"Good morning," she said, her voice still raspy from sleep and muffled against my chest.

"Good morning to you. How did you sleep?"

Instead of answering, she lifted her head and kissed me, causing my heart to soar at the touch.

"Just knowing I could wake up like this made my sleep so much better, but I imagine we'll head out soon?"

I nodded, though it wasn't because I wanted to. As intimate as the moment was, I wished it could last forever, but we needed to get home. I kissed her again, and in one swift movement, I pulled her on top of me—not to take her again, although I wanted to—but just to feel her weight on me for a moment. She didn't object, instead settling her thighs at my sides and wrapping her arms around me. Her scent filled my senses, something both familiar and new.

Before I could kiss her again and become lost in the feel of her skin against mine, someone knocked on the door. I glanced at my mate, huffing out a breath as I moved her to the side and climbed off the bed. I briefly considered answering the door in the nude; perhaps that would deter future interruptions. However, I begrudgingly pulled on my last pair of clean trousers and opened the door.

"I know it's tempting to stay in bed all day with a new mate, brother, but we really should get on the road. It's nearly noon."

If anyone understood what it was like to have a new mate, it was Fionn. He had been away from his own mate and children for a long time, and his son needed medicine. After patting me on the shoulder, his friend turned to walk away but glanced back over his shoulder. "The rest of us are down in the tavern. I'll order breakfast for the two of you."

When I returned to the bedroom, Elianna was already dressed.

A short time later, our group set out. The sun was already high in the sky, and a crisp breeze carried the scent of lavender across the plains. Everyone appeared well-rested, having eaten together at the table before leaving. However, the grins on Fionn and Cailean's faces indicated that our passionate night together had been louder than we had intended. I didn't mind, but it had been enough to make Elianna blush. Given how close Cailean sat to Zoe, I couldn't help but wonder if I was the only one who had made love the night before.

There were only a few hours of travel between the tavern and my cottage—longer if we encountered any unexpected disruptions. We rode toward the horizon, with Elianna safely tucked between my thighs on Shadow's back. The horse had been good to me, and I looked forward to giving her a long rest once we got home. We all needed one.

Zoe still rode with Cailean, her key tucked safely out of sight. With Elianna staying in the Court of Harmony and Cailean returning to the Court of Courage, I wondered what Zoe would choose to do. If she had no interest in the youngest Oathorne brother, the decision would be easy. However, it seemed more complicated, given the unmistakable connection between her and Cailean. I didn't envy the choices either of them would have to make, especially if one of their mates showed up to claim them.

Halfway through our journey, the possibility of danger began to feel more real when Zoe pulled the enchanted object from her pocket. Her face twisted into an expression I didn't recognize as the key transformed into a solid light in her hand. As if it had burned her, she dropped it to the ground.

Cailean's features fell, and Zoe's hands moved to cup her mouth in shock. Pulling on the reins, Cailean stopped his horse and dismounted to pick up the still-beaming key from the ground.

"Don't," Zoe blurted, as if the object could hurt him. The rest of the group halted, watching the exchange, while Elianna drew in a breath and shifted uncomfortably.

"Help me down," she whispered.

After getting off Shadow, I gripped my mate's waist, lifting her from the saddle and setting her on the ground. She quickly dashed over to Zoe, who still sat atop Cailean's horse, reaching for her friend, who was fixated on the key in Cailean's hand.

"Zoe?" Cailean asked, taking a step toward her, the key in his hand held like a smoldering ember. But Zoe shook her head.

"No, Cailean. I don't want it. Leave it here. We can go. Just leave it."

Cailean stood frozen, looking at his father and brother, as if needing their approval to drop the key where he stood, allowing Zoe to walk away from her fate. Elianna tentatively placed a hand on her friend's leg, and my body stiffened when I heard the sound of a horse approaching from behind, the rider still out of view. They needed to keep moving.

I hoped they would.

Drawing Shadow closer to my mate, I kept my voice low. "We can't just stand here. Someone is coming, and I think we all know who it is. If you want to take the key or leave it, Zoe, you need to decide now."

Zoe's eyes flicked up to meet mine, her face crumpling. "I know I'm supposed to feel it when he's near, but I feel nothing for him. The key senses him, but my body doesn't. Shouldn't that tell me something? That he's not mine?"

Unsure of what to say, I focused on the footsteps approaching us. They were too close.

"Maybe it isn't the same for everyone," Elianna suggested, her statement phrased more like a question. "Maybe it's worth meeting him, just to know for sure."

With hesitant steps, Cailean approached, still holding the key in his hand, the light unwavering as he held it up to her. Zoe watched it but did not take it. "If you don't want to go with your mate, you don't have to. We won't let him take you. But please, Zoe, don't leave this day with regret, no matter who you choose."

In that moment, it was clear that Zoe's fear and desire to run transformed into something different—resignation. Holding out her hand, she allowed Cailean to place the key in her fingers before she got off the horse and fell into his arms. The rest of the group moved away, giving the pair the moment they needed. I knew the footsteps were getting closer, Zoe's elusive mate approaching, but we didn't run or retreat. Instead, we waited in the shade of a great oak beside the road, letting our horses graze in the spring grass. Holding Elianna against me, I felt a knot tighten in my chest. My own instinct to protect my mate burned within me, but I couldn't ease it.

As the steps grew louder, I took Elianna by the hand and led her deeper into a grove of trees to hide. It wasn't likely, but if Zoe's mate was part of a group intent on stealing human women, I wasn't willing to risk Elianna's safety, no matter the impact on our friends.

Watching from a hundred yards away, I didn't know who I expected to see when the figure atop a black stallion rounded the bend into view, the illuminated key hanging from the male's neck. What I hadn't expected, and what sent my heart plummeting into my stomach, was a guard in a crimson uniform from the Court of Chaos.

CHAPTER THIRTY-TWO

Elianna

FOUR WEEKS LATER

"Come on, Lazy Bones. Pith has so many other things to do today, and Master Blaze is swinging his sword outside again. Pith doesn't want him to hurt himself, so Lazy Bones needs to go check on him—*immediately.*"

Jerking awake, I opened my eyes to see our new, permanent housekeeper, Mr. Congeniality himself, standing over me. No matter how many times Blaze and I told the brownie to stay out of our bedroom, he still popped in on most mornings, complaining whenever someone was still in bed. I rolled my eyes, kicked the blankets off, and climbed out of bed.

"Pith, how many times do we have to tell you—"

As usual, Pith cut me off with his incessant mumbling. "Lazy Bones never gets out of bed when she's supposed to. Pith only likes Master Blaze, especially when he doesn't wear a shirt. Pith likes his long hair and how he gets out of bed so Pith can do his chores on time."

Holding back my laughter, I slid my feet into my slippers and shuffled out of the room, leaving Pith to his work and his complaining. I knew the light-hearted feeling inside me wouldn't last, but I hoped to enjoy the day at our cottage before we had to leave. With the situation regarding Zoe's mate and the march on Cloudfell to free the other human slaves, we would have to leave our home before the week was over.

Pulling on my cloak as I headed toward the door, I could already see my mate through the windows, indeed wielding his sword against an invisible enemy, shirtless. Pith wasn't the only one who enjoyed the view.

I watched him for a moment—slashing, ducking, and rolling with his sword while the field of crops swayed in the breeze behind him—and smiled to myself. With his flowing dark hair, eyes that shone even more golden in the sun, and a body that could have been carved from marble, he looked like a god. If I'd known this was the male who had been waiting for me all those months, maybe I wouldn't have worried as much and wouldn't have nearly let myself die versus going through the enchanted door.

I thought about my parents often, but my new husband was always open to listening to my stories about them. We even sometimes discussed what it would take for the portal to work both ways and how to find a way for my parents to come through and be with me. It may have only been a dream, but it was a dream worth talking about, worth pursuing if there was a way.

Sometimes, my mate even shared stories about his own family and childhood with me. Once things were settled with the women who needed to be freed, we planned to take a trip to where he grew up. I looked forward to meeting his family and seeing him reunite with them as well. According to Blaze, he hadn't had a falling out with his family, but his time in the war and the work he did for the court kept him quite busy. When he had downtime, he always wanted to spend it at his cottage, working in his fields and enjoying the beautiful landscape.

Now, as his wife and living on that land with him, I understand why he loved being there so much. When the time came and we had children, we found ourselves in the perfect place to watch our family grow. Even at only nineteen years old, being in love with such a wonderful male made me excit-ed to be a mother, whether that time came soon or further down the road.

Turning toward the back of the cottage to take a sip from his waterskin, my handsome husband caught me staring at him and grinned, making me blush. It only took a moment for the back door to open and Blaze to saunter in, sweat glistening on his skin, although the day had only just begun.

"Pith woke me up." Smirking, I walked into the kitchen and put the kettle over the fire. "He was worried you were going to hurt yourself—again."

One of the first things we did when Pith showed up at our cottage was to give him his freedom, although he wanted no part of it. He insisted on being allowed to clean our home indefinitely. We never fully agreed to his proposal, but he still showed up most days of the week, grumpy as ever. He seemed to prefer cleaning the cottage over the manor, since Blaze and I were kinder to him than the lord had been. He definitely preferred it to the abandoned cabin in the woods. Still, the little creature just really liked to complain, and we had gotten used to it, not taking it personally. Whenever one of us mentioned the brownie, he would lend his opinion to the conversation. This time, however, he hadn't, which meant he was probably elsewhere, complaining to one of our other friends.

Blaze chuckled, wiping his face with a rag before leaning over to kiss me. "I don't know why he insists I'm going to hurt myself. I've told him a thousand times that I am a trained soldier."

The kettle whistled, but I ignored it as he pulled me into his sweaty arms and kissed me again, deeper this time. The feeling of his lips against mine filled my body with warmth, pooling low in my belly. By the time I came out of the kiss, I was breathless, and the water had almost completely steamed away.

"Pith should be more worried about me hurting myself. I still need more training." Leaning back to look at Blaze's face, I poked him in the chest. "And you've got to teach me."

We had been practicing controlling and wielding my power since we arrived back at the cottage, but I still needed more practice, especially with using weapons.

Eyebrow arching along with his smirk, Blaze pulled me against him again, the smell of his sweat reminding me of how intense he had been the night before. Twice.

"Let's make a deal." He kissed my neck, tracing his tongue to my collarbone. Shivers rushed through my body, forcing my eyes closed.

"Okay." The word came out as a whispered breath. At that moment, I knew I was clay in his hands. I would have agreed to anything.

Fully aware of the effect he had on me, he lifted me into his arms and walked toward our bedroom, kicking off his boots along the way. "You're too beautiful this morning for me to ignore, my Starlight." When his warm mouth found my neck again, just below my ear, and sucked, I nearly came undone. He only chuckled and kept walking. "So, if you let me take you to bed and make you scream my name, then we can go outside and train as much as you want."

When Blaze lay me down on the bed, there was no need for me to agree to the deal. He already knew my answer. He slid the cloak off my shoulders before pulling off my nightdress. There were no more questions or hesitations between us. After the four weeks we'd been together, we had faced numerous challenges, and our relationship had blossomed into something beautiful and lasting. Even if the key hadn't chosen him for me, I would have chosen him for myself. I would have still loved him for who he was as a person, and for how he treated me, making me feel like the most special thing in the world.

Leaning me back on the bed, he threaded his fingers into my hair, tipping my head back to kiss me, the kiss full of fire. I could feel his heart beating against my chest, the adrenaline from his training laced with lust, powering its movements. He kissed his way down my body, tucking himself between my thighs. The first swipe of his tongue through my folds was deep and slow, as though he were starving, and I was the sweetest fruit worth savoring.

Every time he tasted me, every time we made love, it only got better as we learned what brought the other pleasure, what made the other go wild. Arcing off the bed, my moans echoed through the room as he brought me to the edge quickly, the release hitting me hard, making my body tremble.

When the last shock wave of it passed, I flipped Blaze over onto his back, climbing over him and taking him into my hand. Although I could barely get my mouth around his girth of him, I still enjoyed trying, and he seemed to enjoy letting me. I squeezed him in my hands, his length as hard as steel, and stroked him, taking the crown into my mouth and licking the salty bead on top. My husband groaned, his hips bucking against my hand, encouraging my movements. I worked his length with my hand, my mouth, savoring him, but before he got close, he pulled me up by my shoulders. Rising to his knees on the bed, he settled me over him before pulling me down onto his cock.

There was no longer a tinge of pain when he slid into me. There was only my body begging for more, for him to give me everything, until he wrung out every ounce of pleasure he could from me, until I screamed his name.

With my legs wrapped tightly around his waist, he gripped my hips, surging up to feed his body into mine. Every stroke was electric, his name a worshiping plea from my lips. When I reached my climax again, we went together, left sweating in each other's arms as we tried to catch our breath. When we were done, lying beside each other on the blankets, my leg draped over his abdomen, Blaze chuckled. "I think I got the better end of the deal."

Little did he know, I agreed.

Enjoyed The Other World?

If you enjoyed The Other World, please leave a
review!
https://buy.bookfunnel.com/ep0pppikqh

Sign up for C. A. Varian's newsletter to receive current updates on her new and upcoming releases,
sales, and giveaways:
https://sendfox.com/cavarian

You can also find all stories, books, and social media
pages and follow her here:
https://cavarian.com/

Acknowledgements

This book would not exist without the people who carried me when I couldn't carry it alone.

To my amazing Executive Assistant, Jessica, thank you for helping me keep my head on straight. You make it possible for me to keep this thing going.

To my incredible PA, Aly Dust, thank you for being a creative force and a constant source of support.

To my awesome editor, Willow Oak Author Services, thank you for keeping up with my crazy schedule.

To my super supportive Street Team, your enthusiasm, love, and loyalty made all the difference. You were the wind at my back through every draft.

To my husband, children, and family, thank you for your patience, love, and for understanding that writing a book means sometimes living in another world.

To my readers, thank you for returning to the page,

for believing in keys that open impossible doors, in love that defies worlds, and in the strength of human hearts even in the darkest realms.

Thank you to my cover designers, Artisan Gallery and Artscandare, as well as D'Arte Oriel, for the awesome chapter header design.

From the bottom of my heart, thank you.
XOXO, Cherie

Also by C.A. Varian

Crown of the Phoenix Series
Crown of the Phoenix
Crown of the Exiled
Crown of the Prophecy
Mate of the Phoenix
Shadowed by Prophecy
Shadowed by the Veil (Coming Soon)

My Alien Mate Series
My Alien Protector
My Alien Rescuer (coming soon!)

Other World Series
The Other World
The Other Key
The Other Fate

Hazel Watson Mystery Series
Kindred Spirits: Prequel
The Sapphire Necklace
Justice for the Slain
Whispers from the Swamp
Crossroads of Darkness

The Spirit Collector
The Darkness that Follows (Coming Soon)

The Cursed Waters Duet
Song of Death
Goddess of Death

Survivor & Savior Duet
Saving Scarlett
Keeping Caroline

Standalones
Second Chance with Santa
When Everly Saved Emerald Hollow (Coming Soon
with A.A. Weaver)
Spirit of the Dying Flower
The Gladiatrix & the Fallen Son (Coming Soon)
Wings of the Forgotten (Coming Soon with J. Paige)
The Moon-Cursed Crown (Coming February 2025)

About the author

Born and raised in the heart of Louisiana's Cajun Country, I'm a passionate writer of dark, fantasy, paranormal, and even alien romances—if there's a romance involved, chances are I've written it. My stories are filled with mystery, magic, and intense emotional connections that keep readers on the edge of their seats.

When I'm not writing, you'll find me creating special editions of my books packed with all the bells and whistles—character art, exclusive swag, and more for my readers to treasure. I love connecting with fans, whether it's through my TikTok shop, my website, or in person at events where I can share the stories I pour my heart into.

proud mother and new grandmother, I've faced many challenges in life, including a battle with chronic Lyme disease, but I've never let it define me. Writing is my escape and my passion, and with the support of my amazing assistant Jessica, my husband Trevor, and my daughters, Arianna and Brianna, I'm living my dream of writing full-time. Even my two youngest sisters pitch in, helping me with various tasks for the business—it's truly a family affair!

At home in the coastal region of Mississippi, surrounded by love, laughter, and inspiration, I'm never without my two Shih Tzus, Charlie and Luna, along with my three mischievous cats—Ramses, Simba, and Cookie. Whether I'm doting on my furry companions, reading, or soaking up family time, every moment is a precious one.

Join me as I continue to create worlds full of romance, adventure, and unforgettable characters that you won't want to put down!

9 7989 86 26 3540